HA

ÉDOUARD DUJARDIN (1861-1949), founded *La Revue Wagnérienne* in 1885, in collaboration with his friend Teodor de Wyzewa, and subsequently, in 1886 took over direction of the *Revue Independante*, using his influence to promote Symbolism. He wrote poetry, plays and fiction, his most famous work being the stream-of-consciousness novel *Les Lauriers sont coupés* (1887). Known as a man of refined taste, especially in clothing, and being a habitué of Paris nightclubs, he earned the reputation as a dandy, and is generally thought to be the man featured with the dancer Jane Avril in "Divan Japonais," one of Henri de Toulouse-Lautrec's posters for the Folies Bergères.

BRIAN STABLEFORD'S scholarly work includes *New Atlantis: A Narrative History of Scientific Romance* (Wildside Press, 2016), *The Plurality of Imaginary Worlds: The Evolution of French roman scientifique* (Black Coat Press, 2017) and *Tales of Enchantment and Disenchantment: A History of Faerie* (Black Coat Press, 2019). In support of the latter projects he has translated more than a hundred volumes of *roman scientifique* and more than twenty volumes of *contes de fées* into English.

His recent fiction, in the genre of metaphysical fantasy, includes a trilogy of novels set in West Wales, consisting of *Spirits of the Vasty Deep* (2018), *The Insubstantial Pageant* (2018) and *The Truths of Darkness* (2019), published by Snuggly Books.

ÉDOUARD DUJARDIN

HAUNTINGS

TRANSLATED AND WITH AN INTRODUCTION BY
BRIAN STABLEFORD

THIS IS A SNUGGLY BOOK

Translation and Introduction Copyright © 2020 by Brian Stableford. All rights reserved.

ISBN: 978-1-64525-019-7

CONTENTS

Introduction / 7

Preface / 15
The Devil Helkesipode / 17
The Future Dementia / 31
The Past Dementia / 36
Words of Love / 39
The Dharana / 42
The Story of a Day / 52
The Iron Maiden / 63
The Terror of His Child /68
The Self-Torturer / 74
The Cabalist / 80
A Testament / 87
Hell / 97
The Apostolate / 113

INTRODUCTION

LES HANTISES by Édouard Dujardin, here translated as *Hauntings*, was originally published in Paris by Léon Vanier in 1886. It was the author's first book, published not long after he had founded *La Revue Wagnérienne* in 1885, in collaboration with his friend Teodor de Wyzewa (1862-1917), who was born in the Ukraine but had emigrated to France with his parents in 1869. Shortly after the publication of *Hauntings*, Dujardin took over the direction of the *Revue Independante* from Félix Fénéon, again with assistance from Wyzewa. In the pages of the latter periodical he published the novella *Les Lauriers sont coupés* [The Laurels are Cut] in 1887 (book 1888), on which his principal claim to fame is now based.

Dujardin had inherited a considerable sum of money when both of his parents died, while he was still relatively young—his father had been a sea-captain—and he had no need to make money from his writing, much of which consisted of self-indulgently esoteric works dealing skeptically with religion and lovingly with music, as well as five volumes of poetry. He financed the production of two of his own plays, neither of which was successful, and published one more item of long fiction, *L'Initiation au péché et à l'amour* [The Initiation to Sin and Amour] (1898), but devoted much of his time to social life; he was a renowned dandy during the *fin-de-siècle* and the last phase of the *Belle Époque*, and is generally thought to be the man featured with the dancer Jane Avril in "Divan Japonais," one of Henri de Toulouse-Lautrec's posters for the Folies Bergères.

In the first issue of the *Revue Wagnérienne* Dujardin published an account of Wagner's essays on the theory of art, with particular reference to the relationship between art and religion. In 1887 he followed it up with a longer article, "Considérations sur l'art wagnérien," the introduction to which attempted to generalize the theory and apply it comparatively to the nature and evolution of painting, literature and music. Those studies apparently arose out of discussions between Dujardin and Wyzeva, who also extended the argument in his own essays in the *La Revue Wagnérienne* and elsewhere. Between the two of them they developed a notion of Symbolist Art in which Wagner's work became the key exemplar, but which had wide-ranging consequences, one of which was the notion that prose fiction ought ideally to concentrate intently on the inner life of a protagonist over a limited period of time, ideally no longer than a day—and the suggestion that modern fiction was indeed evolving in that direction.

While he and Wyzeva were developing that argument theoretically, Dujardin was endeavoring to develop and put it into practice in his work, and the early produce of that endeavor is collected in *Les Hantises*, many of the stories presenting searching analyses of states of mind, sometimes drawing extensively on the author's own thoughts and history, in a self-critical fashion. Although *Les lauriers sont coupées* became famous—long after its initial publication—as the "novel" that pioneered the narrative strategy nowadays known as "stream-of-consciousness," *Les Hantises* demonstrates the manner in which the author developed that technique by stages, while using monologues and biographical commentaries as means of analyzing and illustrating the psychological phenomenon of obsession.

Although some of the hauntings featured in the stories in the collection are literal, the apparitions that they feature are liminal, and the narratives are focused entirely on the mentality of the seers rather than the depiction of the apparitions; what haunts the protagonists of the stories is not a supernatural agent *per se* but an idea they have—in several instances, the idea that supernatural agents of some sort might exist. Although there is an entire subgenre of Symbolist fiction that consists of "manic monologues," few examples of the subgenre can compare with the curiosity, intensity and frank perversity of Dujardin's, and although some of his exercises are slight if viewed in isolation, their aggregation in a collection provides a spectrum with a degree of coherency that might be seen as symptomatic itself of mild obsession. At any rate, the collection is certainly not a haphazard aggregation, and its sum offers a degree of insight into the author's personal and philosophical preoccupations at that particular point in his life. It is, however, significant that the author, unlike his characters, abandoned that intense preoccupation with his own inner life and found refuges in society and in more distanced and objective kinds of writing.

As well as being read as a kind of stylistic prologue to *Les lauriers sont coupés*, the collection can also be compared and contrasted interestingly with Teodor Wyzewa's collection of short stories, *Contes chrétiens* [Christian Tales] (2 vols, 1892-93; augmented edition 1902), and it is surely the case that the last two stories in *Les Hantises*—which echo passages and ideas found in Dujardin's theoretical articles in the *Revue Wagnérienne*—were partly inspired and prompted by discussions between the two men regarding matters that interested them deeply, but about which they had to agree to disagree, particularly with regard to religion. Wyzewa translated Jacobus de Voragine's *Legenda Aurea*—known in English as *The Golden Legend*—into modern French in 1902, and his tales, especially the two novelettes added to the second edition of his collection, are in a calculatedly similar vein; they are, however, informed by a markedly different attitude to their substance, almost as if Dujardin's idiosyncratic brand of skepticism were lurking in the background like a sinister scarecrow. In the longest story in *Les Hantises*, "L'Enfer" (tr. as "Hell") the particular bugbear defined and defied by the narrative is scientific materialism, but it is not by coincidence that the story is juxtaposed with "L'Apostolat" (tr. as "The Apostolate"), which closes the collection and by offering a scathing analysis of religious obsession; its bleakly brutal ending forms a sharp parenthetical contrast with the blithely comical tale of academic obsession that opens the series.

Dujardin was by no means the only Symbolist poet to develop a strong interest in the theory of literary symbolism and to attempt to practice it, and his ideas did not find ready acceptance with some of his fellows, who found it difficult to take him entirely seriously because of his affectations of dandyism. Stéphane Mallarmé offered an oft-quoted rude description of him, but entirely in jest; the two were good friends and Dujardin once proposed marriage to Mallarmé's daughter. In any case, idiosyncratic opinions usually form a more interesting foundation for literary experiments than banal ones.

Dujardin's stories sometimes resemble philosophical analyses rather than conventional works of fiction, but they do not aspire to the kind of distanced objectivity to be found in essays; they deliberately go to the opposite extreme, capturing an intense subjectivity, whether in monologues or descriptions of exemplary conduct that insist forcefully on the extreme difficulty—perhaps impossibility—that consciousness experiences in attempting to adopt an objective and rational attitude to sensations. Most people, Dujardin's work observes, do not even try to do that, and he sometimes takes leave to wonder why they should bother—but seen as a whole, the collection leaves no room for doubt that hauntings, even when the haunters seem harmless and impotent, are essentially, and perhaps quintessentially, horrific.

This translation was made from the copy of the 1886 Vanier edition of *Les Hantises* reproduced on the Bibliothèque Nationale's *gallica* website.

—Brian Stableford

HAUNTINGS

PREFACE

Alone, our soul lives . . .
Téodor de Wyzewa

ALONE, the idea is: the world in which we live is our ordinary creation; and sometimes we live in other ideas, other worlds.

On the special creations of life, and the hallucinations of the idea, and a few hauntings—these chapters.

THE DEVIL HELKESIPODE

To Monsieur le Comte de Villiers de l'Isle-Adam[1]

THE first volume of *L'Essai sur l'histoire des traditions démonologiques despuis l'antiquité jusque nos jours* (4 octavo volumes, Paris 1861-65 chez Delalourde, publisher) contained, with the subtitle *Introduction Bibliographique*, a general history of demonology and works of demonology; the other three volumes exposed, in alphabetical order, in the form of a dictionary, the special history of each tradition; and the work was a monument. Having searched incessantly for documents in the libraries of Paris, the provinces and abroad, in museums and collections, in cottages and the most remotes distances, having looked for the residues of ancient legends, scented every trail of the Devil and watched for any demonomaniac shadow, the author had, in accordance with the unalterable rules of the scientific method, noted, compiled, marked, critiqued,

---

1 Auguste Villiers de l'Isle-Adam (1838-1889) was one of the heroes of the Symbolist Movement; Dujardin published two of his stories in the *Revue Independante* not long before his death; "Etna chez soi" (tr, as "Etna in One's Own Home") was serialized in the first two issues that he edited.

compared, divided, classified and systematized; and, impartially, gravely, rigorously and imperturbably, he had described:

the art, power and punishment of demons, according to Jakob Sprenger, the judge of the witches of Cologne, one of the foremost demonographers;

the terrible omnipotent and efficacious exorcisms and remedies to expel evil spirits, according to Hieronymus Mengus (*Flagellum Daemonum*);

"the imposture and deceit of devils, diviners, enchanters, sorcerers, spell-casters, chevilleurs, hieromancers, chiromancers and others who, by means of some diabolical invocation, magical arts and superstitions, abuse the people" (Pierre Massé du Mans, Paris, 1578);

the fifteen terrible crimes of witches enumerated by Jean Bodin;

the evidence that King James I gave of the abominable commerce that witches have with the Devil;

the historical Anti-Demon, in which the spells, larcenies, ruses, and frauds of the Prince of Darkness to usurp the divinity are amply treated (author Jude Sercilier);[1]

also, in accordance with the book by Pierre de Lancre,

---

1 This passage is quoted verbatim from the version of *Bibliotheca Magica et Pneumatica* attributed to the alchemist Johann Grässe (c1560-1623), printed in Paris in 1843. Dujardin might conceivably have owned the book, as well as the Massé title cited, but is more likely to have seen them in the extensive collection of the occultist Stanilas de Guaita (1861-1897), whom he knew, and who contributed poetry to the *Revue Independante*. All the texts cited are real; I have expanded the names of the authors in some cases in order to make them easier to identify.

king's counselor, the incredulity and skepticism of fully convinced witchcraft;

similarly, the account of the various grades of demons, according to Odorico Valmarana;

the description of Hell and the state of the devils before the commencement of the world, according to Antonio Rusca;

the complete exposé, according to Jean-François Sandras, of the pranks of the Devil;

the methods used by the Comte de Gabalis in evoking salamanders, sylphs, gnomes and undines;

how to conjure the Devil and compel the obedience of spirits;

and finally, all the sciences continued in the *Liber Spirituum*, the *Great Grimoire*, the *Great Key of Solomon* and the *Great Black Magic* or *Infernal Forces* of Cornelius Agrippa.[1]

Now, the author—his name was Aristide Genius; he was sixty years of age, was short and thin with an exceedingly bald head and curved back; was Professor of Linguistics at the École des Hautes-Études and of Comparative Mythology at the Collège de France; had three doctorates and wrote in seven languages, not including his maternal tongue—confided one day to his housekeeper that he was about to marry.

The news was passed on by Aristide Genius's housekeeper to the concierge of the Collège de France; immediately, it spread through the classes, among the

---

[1] Cornelius Agrippa did not write the magical handbook attributed to him and falsely represented as the fourth volume of his *Occult Philosophy*.

professors, and then escaped to the Sorbonne and traversed the library of the Hautes-Études in the blink of an eye; from the Sorbonne it slid into the offices of the publisher Delalourde, and then those of the *Grand Revue*,[1] and climbed to the École Normale. On the way it was apprehended by Professor Despointes, who immediately divined by intuition a thousand details, which he related, with gestures, to his colleagues; many others also encountered it and made themselves its messengers. Thus, a few hours after the conversation of the concierge and the housekeeper, there were delicate allusions to it in which people smiled discreetly at the news. That day, the publisher Delalourde sold three copies of the *Essai*.

Why was Aristide Genius getting married?

"He has always lived alone with his old housekeeper; does he desire to change his life?"

"How little you know him! Him, desire a change!"

"Is he bored, perchance?"

"You know that Monsieur Genius doesn't get bored; is it not him who pronounced the famous words: 'Perpetual imprisonment would be pleasant for me with the *Acta Sanctorum*.'"

"Is he marrying because of some ambition?"

"He has no other ambition than science; he lives simply; he scorns wealth and honors; he has a fine salary and income from investments; he's decorated with all the European Orders; people call him 'Master.'"

"Is it a marriage of amour?"

---

1 This publication is presumably fictitious, although a periodical with that title was launched not long after the publication of *Les Hantises*, in 1888.

"Oh, how improbable! Madame is a widow and only twelve years younger than Monsieur."

"Impossible to suppose some secret obligation; Monsieur Genius no longer has any family; in all his travels he has had no adventure. You can't be unaware of the innocence of his mores; Monsieur Genius's eye has never strayed in an unhealthy direction; and the old housekeeper has been able to cry: 'Fortunate Madame Genius! Her husband, with his sixty years, will bring her a soul as pure as an infant in the cradle!'"

Why was Monsieur Genius getting married? Why was that scholarly man, having spent half his life in scientific commerce with Beelzebub and Baal, Pursan, Byleth, Paymon, Belial, Asmoday and Zapon—which is to say, the Emperor and seven kings of the Infernal monarchy—not to mention their court, dukes princes, marquises, ambassadors, generals and militias (they all have their names); having, via books, frequented the Sabbat and visited the somber realm; in sum, knowing, and even knowing intimately, the ancient doctors in theology and demonographer king's counselors, and remaining calm, tranquil, quiet, good, reasonable and happy in the preparation of a fifth volume, a complement to the *Essai*, getting married?

Interrogated, Monsieur Genius replied vaguely.

Well, we who are better informed than the concierge of the Collège de France, Messieurs the professors, the deputy librarian of the Sorbonne, the publisher Delalourde, the editor of the *Grand Revue* and Monsieur Despointes, will tell you the veritable hymeneal story of that scholarly man, who, in his studies, had had scientific commerce with the Emperor and the kings of the Infernal monarchy, frequented the Sabbat and visited Hell, and had even known intimately the ancient doctors in theology and demonographer king's counselors, without losing any of his calm and reason.

Concluding his last voyage of scientific research in Normandy, Aristide Genius passed through the village, interesting to him, of Saint-Étienne-Lallier; there he had the hospitality of a cultivator. It was eight o'clock one evening in September; the days were short then, and coffee was being taken. The table was illuminated by two thin smoky candles. Sitting at the top of the table, among the peasants, in a very good humor that evening and smiling with a grave expression, Monsieur Genius was listening once again, having asked them and directed them to do so, to a confused series of long marvelous stories, always the same. He thought that perhaps he might find a pearl in that mud.

So, he was in a very good humor that evening, for he was smiling gravely; however, not having found the most minimal pearl by the end of the dinner, he grew slightly weary.

"It seems to me," he said, mocking slightly, "that I know the stories you've just told me. Are you sure, my friends, that all those adventures have happened to you and your friends?"

"Oh, Monsieur," they cried, "do you take us for liars?"

"Heaven forbid! It must be, therefore, that the Devil's strategies are the same today as they were three hundred years ago. I'll tell you one that's more extraordinary."

Monsieur Genius was, therefore, very cheerful; he told them the story of a lamia who, after having caused havoc, was expelled by the bishop, a saint. Monsieur Genius had read the story in Jean d'Agnany's book *De Magia et Maleficiis*—unless it was in Benjamin Binet's *Traité historique des dieux et des démons du paganisme.*

"And you saw that yourself?" someone asked.

"If you wish," replied Monsieur Genius—he was joking.

"Monsieur, you're making fun of us; that isn't good."

"No, my friends; my story has for guarantors three royal counselors, two fathers of the Society of Jesus, three doctors of theology and the bishop; it's worth as much as yours. In any case, I wouldn't want to unsettle your faith, fearing the malice of evil spirits."

"Of course, you're a pagan too!"

Monsieur Genius, who chanced to be in a humorous vein that evening, thought he ought to resume his seriousness in order to establish the truth, and with a habitual gesture, putting his hand inside his frock coat, he said: "I'm not a pagan; I respect beliefs; but, having spent my life studying them, I can discern the verity of error; and, taking the part of the beliefs necessary to humankind, I condemn vain, risible and dangerous superstitions."

The good peasants were not accustomed to that kind of discourse; everyone fell silent. In the meantime, the coffee had been drunk, and the darkness was complete. The father turned toward a girl of thirteen or fourteen who was sitting bent over at the extremity of the table.

"Go to bed, child. It's time."

The girl straightened up, without getting up. The farmer repeated the order.

"I see what it is," said the mother. "She's still frightened. Can you imagine, Monsieur," she added, addressing the scholar, "that the silly girl is afraid to go to bed?"

"Of course," said a tall fellow, "with the fine stories she's been rocked with during supper!"

Monsieur Genius, who had gradually abandoned his doctoral manner, intervened. "Tell us what frightens you, my child."

The girl had to be begged; they persisted. The mother promised to accompany her to her room if she spoke.

"Oh," said the child, "it isn't thieves or ghosts. When I have to get into bed, it seems to me that someone, a devil, is going to grab me by my foot . . ."

"What an idea!" they exclaimed.

And the child explained that in the evening, every time that, already having one leg in bed, she was about to lift the other and lie down, she had that fear of having her foot seized by a devil underneath the bed.

Monsieur Genius, still in a good humor, could not help laughing a little, and he made a humorous speech.

"An admirable discovery! A devil who hasn't been discovered by the subtler demonographers and the most expert demonomaniacs! Your daughter, Monsieur, has seen a demon not yet shown to human beings, an unknown member of the six thousand, six hundred and sixty-six infernal legions—and, speaking thus, my doctrine is informed by the book of the *Inventory of the False Monarchy of Satan* by the learned Jean Wierus, nicknamed Piscinarius, a pupil of Cornelius Agrippa, the physician of the Duke of Cleves, who died in 1588; the theory of Godefroy Meyer, who made each infernal spirit a different manifestation of one unique demon is reprehensible and blameworthy in all good demonology. But certainly, whether he is a devil himself or a simple manifestation of Satan, the demon that Mademoiselle has been unable to keep at bay is missing from the lists of all doctors in devilry."

They stared at him. Letting himself go, the scholar—a doctor three times over—continued, still joking: "I have the name of this new tormentor of the human race. In Greek, Messieurs, *helco* signifies pull, *poda* signifies foot; the devil that obsesses Mademoiselle, of whom I am the godfather, is the devil Helkesipode."

When they got up from the table, Monsieur Genius, self-satisfied, promised himself that he would narrate the story to his friends at the Collège de France. The devil Helkesipode! Long live demonology! Godfather of the devil Helkesipode!

And, wrapping his small bony figure in his black frock-coat and blinking his eyes behind his silver-rimmed spectacles, still doctoral and pedantic in his moments of bonhomie, he paced back and forth in the large smoky room, ruminating his words, while, quite astonished, admiring with their bewilderment of country folk, mingled with a hint of mockery, the farmer, the journeymen and the lads in their faded blue blouses and the girls with square hips considered the man from Paris who knew so many things, was so thin, and spoke so well.

Each of them went to his room; the best in the farmhouse had been prepared for Monsieur Genius; he was given a candle and they bid him good night. Monsieur Genius made a few notes, drafted a few lines, reread an article in the *Journal des débats politiques et littéraires* and a few pages of the *Grand Revue*; and, as eleven o'clock sounded on the wooden-framed clock, he began to undress.

In sum, it had been a good day. He had certainly been slightly bored during supper, but he was in a very good mood and he was amused by the final story of the little girl and the devil that grabbed her by her foot in the evening, on the edge of the bed. That was quite unworthy of the essay on the history of demonological traditions from antiquity to the present day; he laughed at it, that pendant. Great minds admit such fantastic relaxations; it is their weakness, if you wish; it suits them. And, taking off his trousers, Monsieur Genius repeated, smiling and satisfied: "The devil Helkesipode . . . ! Godfather of the devil Helkesipode . . ."

Having put on his nightshirt and a cotton bonnet, he opened the sheets and blew out the candle. The bed was very high, in accordance with Norman custom. Slowly—because of his sixty years—Monsieur Genius commenced by lifting his right leg and plunging it between the sheets; at that moment, the idea returned to him of the devil Helkesipode! And as he was about to lift his other leg, in the darkness, he had an imperceptible shudder throughout his body and felt a chill. He turned his head abruptly, with an anxious gaze, toward the floor, under the bed, in the darkness; and very rapidly—

in spite of his sixty years—he lifted his left leg and got into bed. And, bringing the blanket over his head, he muttered: "Am I stupid, then?"

The next day, he left. The farmer found him ill-disposed; in vain the wife asked him whether something had inconvenienced him. The child came to wish him *bon voyage*. Monsieur Genius climbed into the carriage with a brusque adieu.

"Aren't they odd, these scholarly messieurs?" exclaimed the farmer's wife. "Did you see, the rest of you, how he lifted his left leg this morning? He was so polite yesterday!"

"Ideas, caprices, manias," said the man. And everyone repeated that they were odd, those scholarly messieurs.

Monsieur Genius had almost terminated his voyage. He wanted to be in Paris, at home, in the Rue Saint-Jacques. He would not get back until the following day; in the evening he arrived in the small town of Andelys and asked for a room at the Hôtel du Soleil Levant.

His ill humor had not dissipated.

"Damn it!" exclaimed Monsieur Genius. "I'd like to know what's made me so surly! I've succeeded in my research; the weather hasn't inconvenienced me; I'm quite well; I ought to be content; my voyage would have been excellent . . . accursed voyage!"

And, in fact, the illustrious demonographer did not know what was troubling his character.

Soon, he suspected it. For, that evening, while he was taking off his clothes in order to get into bed, the idea came to him, as it had the previous evening, this time without him laughing, with a disturbance of silent anxiety, of the devil Helkesipode.

Was that reasonable? Him, the savant Aristide Genius, the author of the *Essai*, a strong mind! Was that comprehensible? For thirty years he had studied infernal legends; better than anyone else, he knew their absurdity; the Devil had no more mysteries for him; he had played, so to speak, with the horrors of demonomania; and suddenly, such a thought . . .

There are stupidities of which one is not the master—but this one was too much . . .

And, getting undressed, he did not feel tranquil; the devil who had taken the little farm girl by the foot was haunting his mind, strangely.

He did not blow out the candle; and, standing in his nightshirt beside the bed, slightly pale, he gazed again at the floor, he explored the parquet with an anxious eye, seeing he knew not what vague appearance, some mysterious claw ready to seize his left foot when he lifted the right foot . . .

He was afraid.

And, furious with himself, not understanding it at all, asking himself whether he was reverting to infancy or going mad, raging, his mind in turmoil, he cursed his cherished studies, his book, and all demonology.

He was glad to find himself back at home, to rediscover his old habits, his bookshelves, and the good housekeeper who was watching out for his arrival from a window. Dinner was prepared; the regulated hour had been brought forward for the circumstance.

During the evening, a colleague came to see him, with a mysterious expression. After a preamble, he confided to him that the Independent Institute of Sociological Sciences was proposing to award him a special prize for his great work. Monsieur Genius swore that he did not know what that meant; in any case, had he been seen to solicit it? The colleague agreed that Monsieur Genius had not been known to solicit anything whatsoever, and he showed him a few passages from the commission's report:

. . . After the ancient works of history and critical demonology of Thomas Brown, Gabriel Xandé, Hautefeuille and Sauteur, Pierre Lebrun, Lenglet Dufresnoy, Hauber and d'Artigny . . . and we do not cite authors such as Cicero, Pliny, Aulu-Gelle, Apuleius, Lucian, Saint Jerome, Eusebius, Saint Thomas and all the Church Fathers . . . after the modern works of Schartshausen, Harts, Graham Dalyell, Ennemoser, Soldan, Parchappe de Vinay, Brecher, Grässe, Thomas Wright, and Collin de Plancy . . . Monsieur Genius's book, the most complete, the most exact, the most orderly, the most perfect of them all . . .

The highest recompense was due to Monsieur Aristide Genius, the persevering researcher who had never had any other objective than the truth, no other guide than the facts, no other passion than science . . .

A magnificent work that would contribute, was contributing every day, and which had already contributed, one could say, more efficaciously than any other work of propaganda to the emancipation and progress of the human mind . . .

Monsieur Aristide Genius would be considered by posterity as one of the most illustrious apostles of freethought, of positive science and truth . . .

"You've gone a bit far," said Monsieur Genius, shaking his colleague's hand. "I can't accept such splendid eulogies. But I'm touched by your benevolence . . ."

And Monsieur Genius thought about those veritably moving eulogies, and nothing else; then a bitter and tearful thought invaded his mind, for he foresaw that soon, fatally, the apostle of science, the apostle of truth, blemished by an infantile, derisory, inadmissible and stupid dread, the invincible mistress of his senses, dreaming confusedly of instinct, menacing and crouching forms in the silence of the night, by tremulous candlelight, beside an iron bed, would be afraid. In the icy solitude of the bedroom of a confirmed bachelor, on going to bed, he would be afraid of the devil Helkesipode.

THE FUTURE DEMENTIA

IS it an accident, or is it the belated flowering of hereditary seeds? I sense, quite clearly and quite certainly, that I am going mad. At twenty-two, after twenty-two healthy and calm years, I am going mad; I cannot doubt it.

Why did the vain mystery of my youth have to be fatally unveiled? A week ago, I knew nothing about my mother; my father and my father's mother had brought me up; and when I talked about the mother I had never seen, I was told that she had died bringing me into the world; and there were appearances of a lie that I did not understand, and which worried me—but I believed that my mother was dead.

I discovered the deceit. My father received a letter; I was there; I saw him go pale; and, having approached him, I read it at a glance. My father was being informed that his wife had just died suddenly.

I uttered a cry. My mother had just died . . . yesterday, then, she had still been alive; it had been hidden from me; what had they done with my mother? At the same moment, my eyes went to the printed letterhead: *Asylum for the Insane, Ville-Evrard.*

Ville-Evrard . . . asylum for the insane . . . she was mad?

My father replied to me, in a low voice, that my mother had been mad. The illness had taken hold of her not long after my birth; they had been forced to have her committed; they had not wanted me to know about the misfortune.

So, my mother had been mad for twenty-two years and locked away. And I learned that now, never having kissed her forehead, nor smiled at her gaze, nor shown her maternal eye the face of her son.

We departed for Ville-Evrard. I saw the face of the dead woman in her coffin; I thought I recognized features that I had known in dreams. And I thought that I was the flesh of the flesh, the blood of the blood, the life of the life of the dead woman, and of the neglect and the madness, and that my soul was born of the soul that had just died . . .

Certainly, no one has doubted the sanity of my mind; reason, common sense and practicality were my qualities: no excitement, no tendency to get carried away; I was not subject to being struck by an idea, not contemplative; no one could say that I was not a man like any other, one of the crowd, a very ordinary person. How is it, then, that for a week, I have had the sensation that my reason is going astray?

Madness is hereditary, they say. What if I were going mad?

My mother was buried in Ville-Evrard cemetery; my father was present; he appeared to me to be not unhappy, but overwhelmed; one might have thought that a bad memory was weighing upon him. The following night I saw the madwoman again, in my mind; I was awake, my eyes wide open, and in the nocturnal silence, I look toward a corner of the dark room; she was there, as in her coffin, pale, with her eyelids lowered. I was afraid, and I closed my eyes; I could still see her, and I opened them again; I could still see her; she opened hers and looked at me for a long time, and I felt something like a vague breath, her spirit passing into my spirit, her soul descending into my soul.

Oh, my mother, my mother, my unknown mother! Have you left, in dying, have you left to the son that you did not know the somber heritage of your soul and your spirit? Is your breath your mortuary legacy, and the patrimony that is reverting to me from you, after the flesh that you have made me, will it be your mind, your madness, unfortunate madwoman, that you have bequeathed to me in dying? When I went to sleep, at first light, that idea was obsessing my brain cruelly: what if the madness were hereditary, what if I were going mad?

Thus was that night. The next day, I was calmer; I worked, as usual; but suddenly, toward midday, as I raised my eyes, I saw through the window behind the closed panes, in the street, the open coffin, with my mother lying in it, pale, with her eyelids closed; I was delirious.

You can see that I'm going mad. For, in sum, seeing things that aren't there is madness, isn't it? To be pursued by an image, haunted by an idea, and to be delirious, is that not to be mad? A week ago, I was the calmest and sanest of men; could I have been struck like that, without any preliminary symptom, all of a sudden? Perhaps the hereditary madness was lying dormant in my nerves—until the awakening.

Not long ago we were at table; my mother was absent, but my father's face became sinister, his eyes staring, diabolically mocking; evil was brooding in his brow and he was gazing through malevolent eyes full of crimes. Then I had the idea of taking my knife and striking my father full in that accursed face. And I extended my hand, slowly, toward the hilt . . .

Oh, everything will be completed; I shall no longer be able to think; I shall no longer be a man; I shall be irresponsible, devoid of judgment and devoid of will; and I shall become that being, and then I shall have, while awake, those hallucinations, and then monstrous designs will come into my head; it will be necessary to lock me up, like my sad mother.

Let me be mistaken, tell me, prove it, assure me . . .

To sense the evil taking possession of one's being, to sense one's reason falling prey to error, and to follow the loss of one's mind; to be conscious of oneself becoming mad and knowing it; to see the abyss below and to see the heavens up above; to be the inclined surface; to descend and to struggle, clutching at plants and projecting rocks; and to slide, to plunge, to sink, to be swallowed up, with the certain consciousness of one's ruination . . . why did the madness not seize me as an invisible enemy? Why am I not mad enough to be unaware that I am mad? For it is an anxiety, a vertiginous horror to witness the collapse of one's intellect, and to contemplate, as an inactive spectator, as an actor impotent of will, fearfully, the interminable drama of one's thought gradually collapsing.

To be conscious of that is the torture.

Who will tell me that I'm mistaken? I'm right, in this; I'm right, I know that I'm losing my mind; I'm not mistaken, seeing myself become a victim of illusion; my last true sensation is the sensation of my hallucination; my only knowledge is the knowledge of my madness . . . because I am going mad, in full consciousness.

THE PAST DEMENTIA

YES, but one question exists, which mars this happiness. Yes, I'm cured; my physicians have assured me of that; my friends are all expressing their joy in the fact; I know myself that my intellect is assured; I'm cured; I was mad, but I am no longer. But the question is: where am I in my life?

Oh, terrible past in which the lying days of dementia and the veridical days of reason are confused! Between those crises of folly in which I did not believe and the sane calms that I suspected, tremulously, to be deceptive, how can I make the accurate division in my memory? When was that error, and when truth? When was I mad and when was I not? Which were my days of illness, and which were not? What was true and what was false? Of the memories of my life, which are those that I ought to reject as false, and which those I ought to retain as true? I ask myself, in vain: where am I in my life?

My youth was calm, so I was not yet mad . . . but what if that calm was deceptive? That amour, once, was real; those sufferings, those joys, those terrors, real . . . however, I have seen them again, feminine images, and I have suffered amorous torments that were hallucinations; I saw them, those lying images, and I suffered them, those sufferings . . . oh, who can tell whether the former might have been hallucinations and the latter might have been real? Everything was similarly felt, similarly lived, in my flesh and in my brain; so how, now that I'm cured, can I distinguish the truth from the lies in my existence?

One day—I was perhaps twenty years old—I saw a woman who was beautiful, whose eyes were kind, and I loved her. I talked to her, I told her that she was loved. It was in a room darkened by closed curtains, clouded with vapors in which warm breaths floated. And she collapsed in my arms, languidly; she was mine; and our amours lasted, eternally happy. I still have the perfume of her kiss on my lips, and the perfume of her smile in my soul; for she went away, loving me; and she passed from the amorous bed to the deathbed, smiling, beautiful and good.

One day—perhaps I was twenty years old—I saw that beautiful woman whose eyes were kind; I went to talk to her; and in the room—somber, vaporous and warm—where I told her how she was loved, I remember very clearly, her malevolent smile and her mocking voice, and I still have in my eyes and in my soul the vision of the soulless woman.

That woman is the same as the other; it is the same woman that I remember tender and cruel; and I see her like this, clearly, and like that, also clearly. Now, if one was a hallucination, and the other reality, when the memories are indistinctly similar, how can I know which was, and which was not?

It would be necessary to seek material proofs . . . information, what do I know? . . . of how I have lived, of the self in which I ought to believe: where my life was, what I have done, whom I have loved, and what I have suffered, what I was, the self that I ought not to consult; the visions of madness and sanity are mingled in my mind; I'm not a reliable witness; other information is required; and, as if learning the history of some Caesar, I shall go, myself, to study my own history in the documents and memory of others.

O consciousness, self-consciousness! Why, if, I cannot separate true sensation and false sensation in the past, am I not still mad, or why can I recall that I have been?

Yes, I'm cured; yes, but I'm suffering an intolerable anguish, by virtue of having lived, being mad, troubled and deceptive days; and since, conscious of having been mad and having been cured, I must remain in an unenlightenable uncertainty regarding my past, what can it matter to me, for the calm of my present—wretched fellow that I am—that I am now no longer mad?

WORDS OF LOVE

THEY were walking, the two of them, in the remote and almost deserted street of the town, where the shadow of a summer evening was descending; slowly, in the darkening street, traversed by rare passers-by, indifferent or busy; enlaced, looking at one another, and thinking, while he murmured words of love to her.

Oh, the day when she had appeared to him, amid the vulgar luxury of the theater! Him, a poet, deaf to banal harmonies, distracted and pensive—O visionary!—suddenly, he saw her, motionless, beside her sisters, before her father, simple and gentle, the radiant child who retained his venerated name, his wealth and her virginity. Oh, the long days of amour devoid of hope, the waiting beneath the closed window, the heartbreak of encounters without gazes! For months he had followed her, at a distance, spying on her eyes. Oh, the evening when, crossing the square, tremulous and smiling, rosy, she had passed close to him, so that her scattered blonde hair had burned his eyelids. She had noticed him, the young man who glided in her sunlight every day; and, undoubtedly, her childish curiosity eighteen years of age had wondered, secretly, who that pale dreamer was; and doubtless she had smiled at him softly . . . And always, he wanted to dare, but never dared; he had tried to talk to the father: vain visions! Maddened by amour, he had approached her, timidly, on the lookout for a propitious moment, and withdrew, no longer holding the prepared letter, the letter begging for a word of compassion . . .

Now, when he had dared; when she, by virtue of the unreflective pity of her juvenile feminine heart, had come into the isolated garden, he had taken her fingers in his hands; when she had listened to that young man, she had fallen, tremulously, upon his mouth, having heard the words of love . . .

Oh, the words of love, the omnipotent words of love! What are all seductions, compared with those of words of love? You loved, and you went by, unperceived; your intimate amour, in the expectation of a gaze, on the lookout, solitary in your soul; your thought did not fly as far as the heart of the beloved; and the pale flames of your desire drowned in the transparency of her bright eyes. Speak! Words trouble a woman's flesh like a fantastic whirlwind, and cause tumult in its subtle fibers. Words of love are the invulnerable mysterious armaments of the lover.

She, the unknowing, once having listened, as pensively as one contemplates the splendors of a very new world, to the ardent words with which masculine lips had excited her avid ears, was entirely gripped by those mirages, like a child by phantasmagorias. And now, she was walking, pressed between his hands, giving him an hour, a few minutes of every day, and only living in that instant of amour, and for that instant. She found, thanks to the thousandfold resources of her woman's mind, pretexts for quitting the parental house with her governess, a rigid and severe Englishwoman, who followed distantly, a mute confidante; and every time, they went in the shadow of public gardens, beneath the trees of deserted boulevards; she, intoxicated by serene sensuality, confident and respected; he, lost in the infinities of his dreams, forgetful in the chaste caresses of her hair, transfigured.

"Let's stay," he murmured, so softly that his voice floated in the rustle of the evening foliage. "Let's stay like this, in this gaze of our eyes; let's mingle our hands; together, we're together; my mouth is no longer respiring anything but your breath, and I'm drowning in your embrace; and I feel myself fading away confusedly, and my soul, during your embrace, extends all the way to the adorable stars in the sky. O my stainless virgin, my sweet beautiful woman, you are; I love you and you love me, and you are my object and my thought . . ."

At each of those words she shivered, and long tremors wandered from her nascent cleavage to the slender muscles of her fingers; she collapsed, languid and extenuated, in his arms, enfevered by the enchanting words; she swooned, dazed by amour, on his breast, as if a juice were falling from the lips of the young lover, a perfume, a languid and mortal vapor, as if, in a triumphant, invincible, vaguely supernatural intoxication, her woman's heart were expiring of words of love.

THE DHARANA

"IT'S the mental operation known as Dharana; the spirit, emancipated from the world, is fixed in the meditation of Vishnu; then the spirit grasps a sensible form of Vishnu; and, as a fire blazing in the wind ignites thick grass, so Vishnu, seated in his heart, consumes the Seer."

One such seer was Alexis Pranne, the Magician.

One day, Alexis Pranne, having had his mind fixed in the meditation of an idea, saw his ideal Vishnu.

❋

Magic. It is necessary not to disdain anything; it is necessary not to laugh at anything; it is necessary to contemplate everything; science lives outside time and place; seekers are of all the ages; the truth hides from whoever does not desire it with a grave, free and superb amour; the austere truth does not like those who mock. Study things. Study things, for the Word remains eternally. Wisdom was not born yesterday; and for one reasonable century, ours, twenty and thirty centuries could not have been ignorance and folly. Consider the succession of races and empires, peoples and scholars; those thirty centuries of scholarly and popular history; think about human history; all that cannot have been vain, and all is not false of that which has always been. Meditate on what has been; study things; study respectfully, and see.

See what the thought of times was; savants think and people dream; and the thoughts of the former are the image of the dreams of the latter; now, the crowds dream and the sages say one thing; amid human history, one belief; under various forms, religions are the same, and philosophies are the same; all lands, in all ages, are enlightened by the reflections of one light; there is one truth. Asuras, the principle of things; devas, the inhabitants of the distant Sansara; Izeds and Ferouers; Bel and Sin; angel servants of Jehovah and demons servants of Samael; Zeus and his cortege of gods; the infinity of Latin powers; the vague spirit tenants of Scandinavian rocks; mysterious existences, worlds, emanations of Being, which extend, as genii, alternately above and below humanity, unlimited regions, were the belief of the fetishistic savages of the Nile and the ages that cultivated the Pierian Muses. And Jesus taught the expulsion of the evil spirits and the satisfaction of the good; and like the Haoma that gives its faithful its flesh as daily nourishment, Christ offers his body and his blood to humans in sacrifice. Then, those grandiose pressures, the metaphysical divagations of the first heresies, on the fringes of the new faith; the theurgy of Alexandria, the last and most sublime flower of the old trunk of antique religions; Christianity built on the debris of vanished cults; and, from the seething amalgam of universal doctrines to the Middle Ages, the sums of monstrous anxious philosophy, of spiritual agents.

Humans live among invisible spirits, the causes of visible phenomena; that is human belief; Alexis Pranne believed it.

Human being itself is the middle of a chain; nature's work is incomplete therein; it does not conclude with humankind, nor the flight of human being to god; but human being is the median in which, in unified and infinite nature, amid the infinity of the manifestations of one substance, the eternal dissolution of existence into essence, the reflection of the All. Humans are at the admirable point at which the two worlds sensible to human being touch, the two manifestations that human being contains of the manifest infinity: matter and spirit.

Thus, in the world of our realities, there are two appearances of being, which humans unite sovereignly; and something is beneath human being, matter, and something is above it, spirit: below, the inert object, then the animal, in which thought is embryonic; then human being rises, and from the terminus of the body, body and spirit, spirit departs; and higher up in the vague spirit, serene being, and pure spirit. An unlimited sequence of beings, beneath us we see them via our senses; above us, thought sees them; the body sees the body, and thought can see the phantom that commences the spiritual chain, obsessing the human soul with its immaterial wings, the spirit of imponderable form, the subtilized spirit, and all the spiritualities that float outside space, surrounding the human spirit, which matter and the bond enclose.

The spirit knows spirit; the spirit can speak to spirit; the spirit can command spirit. The beings that live without form above our heads can be constrained and subjugated; since the human arm can force obedience from matter, the human spirit, similarly, can force the obedience of fantastic spirits; they are dominated by a powerful will; they bow down to it, and I have them in my servitude if my thought knows the imperious and magisterial word; both material and spiritual nature are open to human will.

Thus, the old science, the primal and universal science, is not vain; it is the sublime science that embraces and contains all others and has engendered them, the eternal magical science.

※

Alexis Pranne had not known his mother, who had died bringing him into the world. She was the last child of ancient noble families of the Franche-Comté, vanished races grave and meditative. The extreme survivor of generations of other faiths, she had been a frail, dreamy young woman, pale and sad, and was said to have been very beautiful.

Alexis Pranne had been brought up in a solitary patrimonial château in the Franche-Comté, almost primitively; he was ignorant of the noisy joys of the early years; a pensive seriousness grew in his brow, like an ancient hereditary legacy. As a child he spent days alone in the solitary plains, while his father dreamed, irremediably taciturn, beneath the vaults of great halls.

Toward his tenth year, Alexis Pranne, having lived in insouciance of the mother he had never seen, thought about that vanished mother. One day, by chance, he found the portrait of a young woman between two pages of a book. His father said to him: "That's your mother . . ."

The book was a Bible; the child read the lines, and having read them, holding the book in his hands, he gazed at the portrait, which gazed at him. He commenced dreaming about the things that one sees, and the things that one does not see.

He had shown an exclusive taste for study at an early age; gradually, he became passionate about it; he did not like any amusement; he was never seen to laugh; there was nothing but study. It soon became relentless toil, without distraction; he never mingled with society. One day, in his fortieth year, he retired to his château in the Franche-Comté and did not emerge again; he lived there alone, finishing his work.

The spirit must respond to the evocative spirit. Thus, there was no book that he had not read; he had learned all languages in order to read all books, and he knew histories, religions and philosophies. He studied all the sciences, and nothing that is human was foreign to him; he knew everything that a man can know; the experience of human generations was reunited in him, and he held knowledge in his hand. Oriental, Hebrew, Arabic and Medieval magic were open to him; he lived the ceremonies of the churches of all lands.

All modern sciences are familiar to a Magician, and he also retains the formulae of the alchemists, the signs of necromancers and the litanies of exorcists. He follows the recent discoveries of astronomers; he reads the movement of heavenly bodies like Leverrier, and the astrological mysteries are unveiled to him. He has repeated the experiments of Claude Bernard, Berthollet and Pasteur; and he has stirred the philters of sorcerers, founded metals, mixed the juices of plants and all the venoms of serpents, and caused sparks to spring forth from stones, like souls. He has known physiological lives and the swarm of inspirations; nature and the demonic world. He has raised himself above the arcana of human psychology and he has repeated the terror of mental invocations. Everything: and in the funereal solitude of his laboratory, amid the impenetrable silence of nocturnal wakefulness, he reiterates everything, seeing appear gradually, during assiduous nights—possible, then probable, and then certain—looming up before him slowly, ever nearer, the law of supernatural evocation.

He follows, from the beginning, the entire chain of universal Magic; one by one, he pronounces every formula and founds every mixture, and in the sublime order of his conjurations, he recites, from the alpha, all the way to the omega, the immense sequence of the prayer that is commandment. And when the final combination appears, the final word, the fatal gesture, the somber unknown of thought will shine, evocatively. Thus, he will have found; Magician, he will be; spirit will obey him.

And Alexis Pranne murmured these words:

"O pitiful human beings, in your ambitions; flesh in which stifled thought groans. To you, money, power, amour: tomorrow, I shall have the word. To you, the rich, the adored, those embraced by women, I abandon my wealth, I live solitary, I have not known woman; virgin of your joys and your desires, alive with the unique spiritual vision, tomorrow I shall have before me my dream made real: the awakened phantom."

Thus spoke Alexis Pranne; and, grave, austere, tall and thin, his head straight and very brown, his pale cheeks shaven, his eyebrows broad and salient, his eyes profound and dark, superbly arrogant in the fixed and vague gaze of a disdainful visionary, when he retired at forty to conclude his labor in the solitude of the final isolation, he had the obsession of the idea marked on his visage, as in his soul.

❋

One evening, Alexis Pranne had stayed awake, and all night he worked doggedly, as he had all day. The end was near.

In his eyes, circled with black, was the increasing anxiety of an immense expectation; his mind, overexcited, embraced infinities of thought in a minute; and it was as if the breath of magical centuries were in his lungs.

Dawn was about to appear on the horizon, but in the laboratory, behind thick curtains, in the shadow of grimoires and retorts, was there any day or night? The pale oil lamp suspended from the ceiling cast gray reflections over everything.

The term was approaching; the idea was about to open. And he thought about his hopes, he thought about the page once open of the very divine Merkabah[1] in confrontation with the maternal portrait, while his hand turned the pages of the final volumes and traced symbols on the walls. Oh, how he had always had, living and ardent, the certainty of the thing! Oh, in that achievement, what anguish and joy there was! And his being was exultant while the term drew nearer: Magician, he would have spirit, the superhuman world, before his sovereign will; spirit, the material, manifest, phantom . . .

The lines joined; the mystic triangle was closed, circumscribed in the circle; visible in the entanglement of signs, the letters expressive of Thought gleamed . . .

Acrid vapors, in green-tinted gusts, floated in the great nocturnal silence with a faint crackle. Having no more to do than rise into Thought, he paused momentarily and before completing the action, during a second of dream, he stood still, leaning lightly against the wall, under the fear of what he was about to do; all his life, all the life of the universe, came into his soul.

At that moment, outside, dawn broke, virginally perfumed, at the tops of green April trees; in the distance the railway line was designed between the clumps of bushes, and the night train from Paris to Belfort drew nearer.

---

[1] The Hebrew Merkabah (Dujardin renders it Mercaba), in the context of mysticism, refers to the chariot of God seen in prophetic visions, most notably the one featured in chapter 1 of the Biblical book of *Ezekiel*. It became the symbol of an entire school of Mysticism.

In the little station, a troop of hunters descended; they were arriving unexpectedly, cheerfully, having planned to surprise Alexis, a friend who had forgotten them, and to depopulate his forests. They made haste, with the cries of awakened sleepers, counting and calling to one another; gripped by the morning air, they were laughing in advance at the astonishment of the tenebrous fellow; they inhaled the spring breeze and considered the rosy whiteness of the dawn joyfully.

And in the night, the night of aromatic mixtures, fuming crucibles and open grimoires, in the bleakly lunar night, and the silence barely troubled by a faint crackle, by the prodigious terror of magical preparations, the Magician, very pale, with flamboyant eyes, very feverish, with dull eyelids, had straightened up, looking straight ahead, into the void of the shadow, and he took a step forward; with his left hand he touched a Biblical book, where words were ringed by a line: "I see visions . . ." And with his thumb he brushed the portrait of a young woman—pensive, pale and sad, and very beautiful—and in his mind, heightened by the power of the will, obstinately fixed, he pronounced the thought of evocation.

Then his short black hair, having become whiter than the snow of the mountains, stood up upon his head; his eyes protruded from their frightfully dilated orbits and his breathless breast capsized; his abdomen tightened; his throat became suddenly dry; his heart stopped beating and his spirit was petrified, for a minute that was a million centuries, outside time.

For if, later, after breaking down the door, they found, near the wall, a living corpse devoid of thought, an inert being devoid of will, it was because he had had his hallucination: in that moment, standing, motionless, his gaze in the profound void of space, suddenly, he saw, he saw with his eyes, before him, present, real, without error, without illusion, he actually saw something, distinctly, clearly, certainly, a shadow, a phantom, a spirit devoid of form but sensible, devoid of color but apparent, an upright specter that was gazing at him.

THE STORY OF A DAY

MAURICE DUPONT gets up between seven and eight o'clock, and never wonders what he will do during the day, knowing that perfectly well in advance. Maurice Dupont, twenty-three years of age, is a student in law, with a paternal allowance of a hundred francs a month, and the junior clerk of an advocate, with a salary of a hundred and fifty francs a month, and, although from Isigny, very Parisian, Maurice Dupont was born to shine in the splendors of the kingdom of the fops and to appear by turns cool, smart and snappy, ringing bells; he cannot escape his necessary vocation, but Maurice Dupont, the son of a worthy provincial merchant is a student, an advocate's clerk with a monthly income two hundred and fifty francs, and he cannot follow his vocation.

Now, Père Dupont had earned, in Isigny, an income of a few thousand francs by means of commerce in butter. He only had one son; he was sent to college; he won all the prizes; it was known, by that token, that he would be a great man. There had never been any question of putting him into butter as well; the idea of giving him a mercantile trade was soon rejected. Young Maurice was proud; his parents understood that. In the end, not seeing any professional penchant in him, he was taken as far as the baccalaureate, and there was talk of liberal careers; Maurice Dupont declared that he wanted to be an advocate.

He had been taken to Paris four times, recompenses for his success. He desired to do his law in Paris; studying in Caen or Rennes was repugnant to him. But he was obliged, to begin with, to submit to military service; he was sent to Courbevoie; he often went to Paris, and knew the monuments of Paris, but the barracks sickened him; he became prouder. At the end of autumn he returned to Isigny and prepared for his definitive departure. One morning in November, carrying two trunks of clothes and a crate of books, having embraced and discreetly consoled his father, he climbed into a railway carriage with his mother, who was to install him personally.

As he did not want to live in a furnished hotel, a room was rented on the sixth floor overlooking the courtyard, in a little street in the Saint-Germain-l'Auxerrois quarter, at a price of a hundred and twenty-five francs a year. A few items of old furniture were sent from Isigny, a few bought for the occasion. Maman departed; the young man set to work. The following summer he passed his end-of-year examinations, fortunately, and was entered into the office of an advocate. However, having a sociable character, he had linked himself with a few comrades from the École de Droit. Maurice Dupont was proud, but he was prudent; he chose for friends young men who were not rich and not poor, but well-turned-out. Then, by means of their frequentation, reading and walking, and especially by means of the theater, during his early years, he learned what Parisian life was, and gradually familiarized himself with fashionable elegance—fashions of speaking, acting, dressing and thinking, and he was initiated into chic.

So, since it is necessary to relate one day in his life, Maurice Dupont, who has been in Paris for two and a half years, and who will be an advocate in a few months, gets up between seven and eight o'clock. His toilette lasts for three quarters of an hour; the care of his toilette occupies half of Maurice Dupont's thoughts; his maxim is: the habit makes the monk. He is almost small, but in his person he is rather well-built; he is slim, for which he applauds himself; he has the good fortune to have delicate hands; his short-cropped hair is very dark, and he wears a thin, very dark moustache; his eyes are not large and their color is vague, but they are profound and the lashes very long; the nose is thin and the mouth ordinary, with thin lips—an aristocratic cachet. Finally, he is myopic, sufficiently to use a lorgnon without actually needing one. He is dressed by a good tailor in the Rue de Richelieu, who becomes a great tailor in his discourse, and his boot-maker has three clients in the Jockey Club.

Every day of the week is worthy of the same elegance. At eight-thirty he goes down the six flights of stairs, absolutely correct and fashionable, clad in his very tight jacket, swinging, without affectation, a cane with a gilded pommel. The neighbors, workers and petty employees, and the concierge, whisper as he goes past, while, with the detached and bored expression that is the height of good form, he heads toward the advocate's offices in the Faubourg Saint-Honoré.

And, crossing the streets without getting any dirt on his boots with pointed toes and broad heels, he thought that people were surely wondering who that gentleman was, out for a morning stroll . . . that outfit suited him rather well, but how hard it was! Another five francs eight-five at the laundry this week. The laundry was killing him. Bah! He knew how to catch up. A horseshoe on his plastron was necessary; sportsmen were beginning to wear them.

And he arrived in the Faubourg Saint-Honoré, at the office. A chic quarter . . . since he couldn't offer himself a suitable apartment, it was better to keep the poor sixth; he didn't receive anyone there; he gave the address of the office . . . it had a grandiose air, that office . . . people from the highest life among its clients . . . junior clerk! But the most launched young men do their law; it's the profession of everyone who has none. To be an advocate's clerk is an obligatory stage for anyone occupied with law at all seriously; one can occupy oneself seriously with the law, that is accepted . . . in sum, nothing that is not admissible.

From nine o'clock to half past eleven, he generally stayed in the office; sometimes he went out on business; then there was always a similar embarrassment: the file that he had to carry, should it or should it not be hidden inside the overcoat? There were prodigies of skill in the way he went forth lightly, holding the cane with the gilded pommel in his right hand and the overcoat in his left, with the invisible file. And while he walked, Maurice Dupont thought about what people would think of him.

He was almost always seen on foot, never in a cab; he had a horror of cabs. He said: One goes on foot or one goes in style. He accepted the railway for the outskirts and the suburbs; he was seen on the imperial of a tram, standing up, leaning negligently on the balustrade; and, having shown admirable ignorance there, he said that one could travel, but not sitting down, in the imperial of a tram; he had seen several gentlemen there; it was done that year.

At half past eleven, breakfast at the office; that was the painful hour of the day. The advocate had to furnish his clerks with bread and wine; they had to buy breakfast at a nearby soup-kitchen and eat it together in the main room of the office. Maurice incessantly had the anxiety of being surprised during that breakfast, differing little from those at the Maison d'Or. The meal was brief for him; while the other clerks chatted, noisily, and took their time, he, unalterably correct, spoke little and hastened. Among the young clerks, he frequented one, the senior, another that one could also encounter, and a third who was presentable, at the extreme of rigor; as for the rest, one scarcely dared salute them in the street. To justify the rapidity of his meal, Maurice had the pretext of a lecture course; when the course was concluded he returned slowly to the office; he did not go into a café; it was not an hour when one ought to be seen in a café; and he did not admit unnecessary expense.

The afternoon in the office; friends sometimes came to see him there: the three or four elegant comrades from the École, not rich and not poor; and a few others: a young painter who gave him anxieties; already known, second medal at the last Salon, with artistic and also worldly relations; a serviceable fellow and an agreeable commerce, that precious friend reeked strongly of Bohemia in his attire. Maurice had tried to bring him to conventional mores—wasted effort; he only required correction, though. And, torn between the desire to continue a pleasant and useful friendship and the annoyance of being seen with a person who neglected himself, Maurice Dupont compared his embarrassment, obligingly, with that of a prince giving his arm to the daughter of a millionaire baker whom he is marrying, and whom he loves.

Finally, at five o'clock, the best part of the day commenced; having had his boots polished by the concierge at the office, Maurice went downstairs and, inevitably, unless the weather was very bad, headed toward the boulevard. To begin with, a quarter of an hour of vague strolling; Maurice knew how to walk like a perfect dandy; in his attitude there was disdain, ennui, nonchalance, affectation, arrogance, politeness, ease, stiffness, humor, correction and impertinence.

Then he stopped at some grand café, preferably the terrace of Tortoni's, and he ornamented it for half an hour. Not that he knew any of the regulars; he would have liked to try to approach a few fops but, sensing the lightness of his purse, he prudently did not dare; and on the fashionable terrace, among that mixed public of the high-life and the rich, he remained alone, his legs crossed and straight, body tilted back, playing with his cane and staring ahead, indifferently, very glad when a friend, someone known, perceived him as he passed by, or some distinguished client of the office, some important person once seen, who returned his salute and who had forgotten his name.

On some days, a friend accompanied him, most often the chief clerk, a young man almost as remarkable as Maurice, but having the snag of thinking about literature; he wrote very paltry tales for a revue. They sat down together; then Maurice talked, with a cigarette in his lips, in unfinished sentences, discoursing about social gossip that he had read in *Gil Blas*, premières that he had allowed to pass, demi-mondaines whose names he knew, the racecourses that he frequented on Sundays and the reception at the Jockey Club of some comte or other. Then, with a distracted ear, he listened to his friend confide to him the subject of his next short story, encouraging him at intervals with little interjections of "very good, my dear!" and when they got up, he said that he would be spending the season at the sea-baths at Isigny, with his family.

At six o'clock he went home, and before going in he traversed a narrow street behind Saint-Germain-l'Auxerrois, and, rapidly, correctly, he bought a little bread, a little cheese a slice of roast pork or some other cheap meat, and, putting it all in the pocket of his overcoat, he went back up the six flights of stairs. Sometimes, a basket of provisions arrived from Isigny, and a few pounds of butter.

Often, in the evenings, he stayed in his room to work; then, the laws of chic became obscured in the shadow of juridical volumes; and at night, lying in his iron bed, before going to sleep, he dreamed about the future. Soon, he would be an advocate; to begin with, he would not quit the office, a minimal resource; but he would try to obtain cases; what a brilliant destiny . . . a fashionable advocate . . . and he went to sleep, glimpsing the luxurious study, all quilted, where the intimate confessions of beautiful blushing socialites died away . . .

Often, also, having dined rapidly, he got dressed again. To go out for the evening was his great desire, but he got very few invitations; the four or five soirées of his employer—rather bourgeois soirées, at which he secretly rejoiced—and two or three others picked up here and there . . . a fashionable man cannot abstain from going to soirées, and, talking to his friends, he told them how tedious soirées were . . . a mortal invention, that one . . . but one could not liberate oneself from them and refuse them all; it was necessary to resign oneself.

There was also the theater. Impossible for him to appear in mediocre seats, so he often paid for good ones; by virtue of a few acquaintances, facile for a Parisian, he was able to show himself gratuitously on occasion at the Vaudeville, the Nouveautés and the Opéra; always in formal attire—one only goes to the theater in formal attire—black cravat, faille and satin, monocle suspended from the waistcoat; if he was distinguishable from fashionable men it was by the perfection of his elegance and the refinement of his dandyism.

Occasionally he offered himself another recreation, having put on a white cravat with his frock-coat, at the time when people were coming out of the theaters, alone or with a conniving friend, in the midst of idlers, prostitutes and night-owls, utterly irreproachable, he strolled along the boulevards.

And coming back from a soirée, or the theater or the boulevard, on foot—one goes by foot or one goes in style—wrapped in the overcoat, from which discreet perfumes exhaled, the simultaneously bitter and sweet reflection came to him: who would think that that accomplished gentleman is a poor junior clerk to an advocate, a native of Isigny, two hundred francs a month? And it happened that while walking, he weighed in his pocket the two or three louis, sometimes ten francs, sometimes a single ten-sou coin contained in his purse, bought for twenty-five francs at the Palais-Royal.

Then, going past the Maison Dorée, the façade and glory of which he knew so well, he watched—without stopping—the bare-shouldered demi-mondaines coming downstairs, for whom he would have been a perfect cavalier . . . But he abstained from women; the initial impetuosity of his arrival in Paris had been satisfied obscurely, with streetwalkers picked up in the Latin Quarter; having calmed down, he judged unworthy of him the fantasies that were sufficient for his friends; unable seriously to aspire to a liaison in society or the demi-monde, he renounced the possibility.

He had imagined, at first, that he might perhaps succeed with a demi-mondaine, by virtue of a caprice; such a liaison would have opened doors to him and positioned him. Once, he had set his sights on a dancer at the Opéra, a leading player who was no longer young and whom many thought ugly. He had perceived her, by chance, in a rather modest restaurant where she dined habitually with a bald American consul; thus his passion was born. Having followed her for a month with a mute and distant court he found a means to be introduced to her; he was well received, and risked a declaration, the effect of which was despairing.

After some hesitation and research, he permitted his heart to catch fire for a demi-mondaine he met one evening at the Vaudeville, and whom he escorted from the theater as far as her carriage; the next day, he went to see her; he was unable to pose as a formal suitor, and, in the meantime, obtained obliging smiles; he was admitted to offer his homage. After a few days of a very pure liaison, he calculated that he had spent a month's money on inconsequential bagatelles; he employed the pretext of a voyage, gave up, resignedly, and consoled himself in solitude.

From those two adventures, however, he gained a precious advantage: being able to talk about two beauties, and salute them on a few occasions, in the company of a friend.

Oh, when the time came, when, as a fortunate advocate, he would be received, sought after and pampered in elegant society . . . ! Today, a student and an advocate's clerk, devoid of a name and relations, appearance contented him; he adopted the attire, the manners, the language of the ideas of society; he pleased himself with the imitation; he delighted in the simulation and enjoyed the illusion; and, perfectly similar to the most exquisite socialites, in generic theaters, fashionable cafés and the corridors of the Opéra, amid subscribers, millionaires with mistresses in the corps de ballet, at the exit, under the rotunda, among the wives of ducs and bankers, in that brilliant crowd, absolutely unknown, Maurice Dupont dreamed that he was part of that world.

And sometimes, remarked for an instant for the distinction of his costume, he imagined that he was one of those dandies, and that he too, flattered and envied, would bear illustrious nicknames—King of the Swells, the Flower of Chic, the Essence of Cool—and superbly fashionable, he smiled internally at his regal glory.

THE IRON MAIDEN

To Edouard Rod[1]

A woman said to me:
"Sometimes, the men who love us, and belong to us, escape us; suddenly, as we are talking to them, we understand that their gaze, momentarily vague, is going into the void; while we are adjusting a curl of the hair, their mind has flown far away. What do they see with that haggard gaze? What new sensation, what new idea, has fascinated them? Then everything has dissipated; the nasty vision is effaced, and there they are, smiling, tender and attentive. But we're troubled and anxious, because we don't know into what chimerical region they went a moment ago, and we tremble, thinking that they have returned to us amid the frisson of an unknown profundity."

Thus a woman spoke to me. After a moment of reveries, I replied to her:

"Yes, sometimes, an extraordinary vision surges forth abruptly, clearly, before my eyes; and the terrible clutches my soul and slides into my blood, my marrow. My

---

1 The Swiss-born novelist Édouard Rod (1857-1910) was editor of the *Revue contemporaine* in the mid-1880s.

nerves and my muscles; and I remain still, in a vertiginous fixity, prey to an atrocious intoxication, drunk on anguish; then, as a spark is extinguished, it vanishes—only later, indecisively, the memory comes back to me, like a dream. But I retain in my soul the terror that, if the vision had been prolonged for a quarter of a second, my reason might have succumbed to the delirium of the hallucination."

We fell silent. Then—it was in a corner of an artist's studio—a man who was sitting with his head inclined toward his knees raised his head. His back was stooped, his cheeks pale and hollow, his forehead wrinkled and his hair gray, but he did not seem to be an old man. He was tall and thin; his garments were elegant and his bearing negligent; his eyes, very dark, seemed extinct, but when he was animated they had glints. At times, a very disdainful smile parted his lips; his body remained folded, leaning forward, his arms crossed over his thighs, devoid of gestures; his voice was slow, with ironies; in sum, while his gaze lit up, it was a somber transport. He said to us:

"Listen to the story I'm going to tell you; and if it comes to your mind that my hero is me, well, keep or reject that opinion as you please.

"Since he had abducted her, my hero, a young man, had been traveling the world with his beautiful mistress; they were two true lovers who paraded their joyous insouciance together from city to city. They wandered in the voluptuous scenery of Germany, having crossed the heroic banks of the Rhine, the gentle hills of Baden and Mayen's melancholy valleys; now they were dreaming in the cheerful old streets of Nuremberg, of the sweet amours of olden times.

"That day they were going to see Nuremberg Castle.

"On the sunlit road, close by, foreigners were walking in a little caravan; by a few overheard French words they recognized compatriots; they were two young women with their husbands; they joined them. And all of them, chatting and laughing, climbed up slowly, two by two, following the enormous walls, where the pink umbrellas and furbelows were reflected.

"The castle had been made into a museum of instruments of torture; the multiple apparatus of ancient excruciations was all there; there were racks, wheels, pincers, swords and bellows, terrible and bizarre engines. While considering them, Lucy clung more tightly to her lover's bosom; he squeezed her white hands; and under those vaults, thinking about the wretches who had once howled in those tortures, they looked at one another, silently tender, and their pity reawakened their amour; kisses wanted to touch their lips.

"The guide took the tourists into a dark chamber; after a few seconds, in the center of the room, a human form became distinguishable in the shadow, upright and crudely modeled: a statue in wood and iron, a woman in a large rigid cloak. The guide made two doors turn, which opened forwards in the middle of the statue, showing in the interior the place of a man. The walls and the two battens were bristling with long iron spikes; when the doors were closed, those spikes were intended to pierce and tear the eyes, cheeks, flanks and whole body of the condemned man.

"The little troop of Parisians fell silent, and Lucy hid her eyes behind her gloved hands; she let the quivering arch of her back fall into her lover's arms while he, sustaining her and inhaling the warmth of her hair, gazed at the monster. Then, pulling herself together, she raised her eyes again, shook her head, and suddenly, noisily, burst out laughing. She proclaimed that, after all, it was too much.

"She had drawn nearer, the young beauty; negligently, she made a tour of the statue, slapping the sanguinary wall with a glove, and with the tips of her fingers, jokingly, she tested the sharp points, not blunted after centuries of usage. In a mischievous manner, she posted herself before the opening, leaning forward, inspecting the interior, and as the whole troop was amused by her playfulness, boldly, childishly, with the petty bravado of a naughty little girl, in spite of the remonstrations of the guide, she stepped inside, nestled against the terrible flanks, and under the thrusts of her umbrella, her pink and white skirts stuck to the narrow iron wall.

"'Close it,' she said, 'and it will all be over.'

"And, facing her lover, she was a laughing figure between the two open arms of the colossus, like an unclosed coffin, ready for the torture. Her lover, who was trying gently to hold her back, and calling her foolish, and scolding her, saw her thus.

"Then a vapor passed over his brain; it seemed to him that he saw the iron maiden close her arms. He seemed to see the iron maiden close frightful arms, and that she closed them on his adored mistress, and that she clasped her, piercing, tearing and crushing her soft, frightfully shredded flesh between the sharp points; he perceived the horror of the gaping wounds, the burst eyes, the perforated breasts, the blood pouring from the cherished loins as if from a sieve; grimacing, the face of his beautiful lover appeared to him ignobly, a spike staving in the mouth that kissed him; and that beautiful body, which he covered feverishly with his lips, that beautiful perfumed body, which exhaled all enjoyments for him, by virtue of that instantaneous vision, he believed he saw kneaded by the fingernails of the Maiden of Maidens; and—a mystery of the magic of the soul—in that hideous contemplation there was such a fascination, such a ferocious voluptuousness, such an infernal and diabolical joy, his being was intoxicated to such a degree by the idea of her doomed and him damned, such was the extraordinary inebriation of that thought of frightful suffering, that with a savage, hoarse cry, the precipitated himself upon the monster, and with his two hands, closed upon the adored mistress the mortal embrace of the iron maiden."

THE TERROR OF HIS CHILD

At twenty-six years of age Anatole Chomet had his first long passion: a little brunette milliner with large dark eyes. Anatole Chomet was a sales assistant in a clothing store; he was reputed to be an honest and laborious fellow, and he rejoiced in the evening in going back to his mansard with his mistress.

One day, she told him that she was pregnant.

Everything was kept secret. The fatal moment arrived; the childbirth was terrible; a daughter was born, and the mother died.

Anatole Chomet, finding himself alone with his child, was afraid. It was an evening at the end of March; the trees were beginning to turn green. Having wrapped up the newborn, he went out, and went to deposit her surreptitiously outside the door of a hospital.

The next day, he returned to the shop; and gradually, by means of hard quotidian work, he forgot. But he did not take another mistress. He told himself, in any case, that it was necessary to think about his fortune. He set about making up the time and money lost. He worked doggedly.

Anatole Chomet was intelligent and lucky. He was able to be honest enough to conciliate general esteem.

At forty he was the head of a large commercial enterprise, and he prospered; thanks to skill and fortunate operations, he made a great deal of money.

Then he thought that he could change his life. Since his twenty-sixth year, laboring ardently and indefatigably, he had savored neither pleasure nor repose. Now that, like the others, he was rich, he had hours of leisure and amusement. For long enough he had gone pale in dusty warehouses and solitary rooms; he would lead a joyful life; he too would have women and horses; he ought to forget the days of difficulty, ennui and stubborn saving; he wanted his armchair at the Opéra, damn it, and to put his arm round the waists of the demoiselles in the corps de ballet; he would sup in the Café Anglais and join a well-known club.

Monsieur Chomet sketched, in his head, the plan of his new happiness. He was no longer the tall lanky fellow of old; he had a paunch, wore side-whiskers, would show himself to be a fine fellow, and promised to be generous. At forty-five, able not to admit more than forty, rich as he was, devoid of chains, he would finally amuse himself, without having stolen it.

Just then, it was the epoch of the carnival; he found friends, fashionable men, to whom he offered dinner. Together they deliberated fitting out Monsieur Chomet's new life. A man of letters who had long hair introduced him into a very visible circle; the brother of a celebrated actress promised him a good subscribed armchair and agreeable relations; they did not fail to have him dressed at Dusautoy's and to choose him a little coupé at Binder's; the dappled horses came from Comte

Alphonse de Gréquenville's stables. It was decided that Monsieur Chomet's entry into the world of amusement would be at the last Opéra ball

Anatole Chomet had never been to an Opéra ball; he was amused. The man of letters explained the organization of the fête to him, and the brother of the celebrated actress designated to him, in a casual fashion, a few beautiful demi-mondaines as well as the most remarkable of the costumed women of easy virtue. The excellent Chomet laughed heartily in putting his finger in the back of those disguised individuals, as the man of letters obligingly taught him to do. At three o'clock in the morning Comte Alphonse de Gréquenville joined the friends, and introduced Monsieur Chomet to a pretty little brunette in white satin, masked by a lace mantilla. She took his arm; other couples formed; they left and went to supper at the Riche. Monsieur Chomet learned that his companion was known by her forename, Mademoiselle Neni, and that amused him; he found her pleasant and told himself, internally, that she was doubtless very young. In his quality as a newcomer, he wanted to pay for the supper himself; that benevolent procedure was remarked by the ladies; Mademoiselle Neni permitted him to take her home.

He was a little embarrassed, penetrating into the dainty entresol, well upholstered, warm and perfumed; but, as a man of intelligence, he strove not to allow anything to show, and, with his heart full of joy, his eyes lit up and his hands burning, he sat down on the divan beside the beautiful girl. Being fatigued, she had not taken the trouble to take off her mantilla; she was tipped back on the cushions, in a studied nonchalance, only allowing the pink tip of her nose and her large dark eyes to be perceived. There was something infantile and delectable about her that charmed him; and Chomet recalled the sadness of other times, seeing rich carriages pass by. He took the child's hands, drew nearer to her, and exhorted her to remove her mantilla.

With a flick of her hand, Mademoiselle Neni threw it into a corner and appeared, laughing. Chomet considered her, with an admiration mingled with joy, and the flux of his desires made his temples throb. With a gallant word he hazarded an arm under the supple arched waist.

"Oh! What are you doing, Monsieur?" she said, with a little moue, but without pushing the bold arm away. "You've been very gracious to bring me home; now it's necessary to bid me adieu."

At that moment, a clock chimed six o'clock. Neni got up and thought: *Friday* . . .

It was her birthday, she had been born with the spring.

"Guess my age . . . you can't? Well, know that it's eighteen years." She continued, laughing: "You're astonished that I know my age so exactly. Eighteen years, Monsieur! I'm no longer a child; I'm a woman. You don't believe me? But what's the matter? Truly, there's nothing very astonishing . . ."

In fact, Anatole Chomet had stood up; and, finding in the face of the young woman something vaguely familiar, he looked at her more and more intently, going pale. And he was motionless, repeating, in a very low voice: "Eighteen years . . . March . . . those eyes . . ."

For suddenly, a whiff of a distant, forgotten time, the absurd thought had reared up in his mind, surging forth abruptly and unexpectedly, like something buried alive, which was presumed to be dead: *Her*.

In sum, that freak of chance was possible. Nothing proved that it was the case, but it was possible. No reason, no indication, no sign, no mark gave it a probability, but in sum, it might be the case that she was his daughter. And he considered, haggardly, that woman with parted red lips, ready for his lips.

Then, madly, he recoiled, and, stammering incoherent words of apology, leaving Mademoiselle Neni stupefied, he departed. It would be too horrible, if she were his daughter.

And he went home, obsessed by the absurd thought.

In the days that followed he was sad, the vague doubt poisoning and spoiling his life. He dared not go to see the woman; how could he confess the suspicion? In any case, what could he have learned? In secret, he sought information, and discovered nothing.

He had refrained from telling his story to his new friends; he made a violent effort, and contrived to set it aside; he proved to himself that he was a great fool to be troubled mentally by a chimera, and even to have arrested the course of his good fortune himself, at the crucial point. A new party was organized, without Mademoiselle Neni.

Monsieur Chomet was introduced to a blonde demoiselle, and obtained in advance permission to take her home, promising himself, this time, to profit from the opportunity. But then, as he looked at that joyous young woman, and thought of that smiling beauty that he was about to possess, that tender grace—that youth—the absurd thought returned to him, to give her up. He wanted to destroy it, but it remained, inexorably taking possession of his mind, victoriously.

What if this one were my daughter?

With the result that he was stupid in the midst of merry friends. Sometimes, his preoccupation was noticed; the man of letters with the long hair teased him very gently. "What is Monsieur Chomet thinking about? Balancing accounts, no doubt? He's forgetting his companion." And the poor man tried to smile, but soon he forgot everything except for the beautiful companion who might be his daughter.

Oh, the child, abandoned in a cowardly fashion, long ago, at the door of a hospital, the daughter of his flesh and his amour, his child, what had become of her? A young woman now, where was she? Oh, the child eighteen years old, where had the hazard of destiny thrown her? And he would never know what had become of his daughter; never, perhaps seeing her, would he know her; for him, her father, she no longer existed, she would never be anything but a girl passing by. O common fate of abandoned children! For it might be that she was one of these women of amour, his daughter, a prostitute, and perhaps he had encountered her some foggy evening; he might encounter her; she might solicit him to follow her; and perhaps that was her, there, who was supping, her cleavage naked, offering her body, whom he ought to kiss.

Somberly, he went away, alone, through the swarming crowd of belated night-owls.

THE SELF-TORTURER

To Joris-Karl Huysmans[1]

"SUFFERING is also a joy," a man said to me, while, leaning on his elbows at a table in a brasserie, he played nonchalantly with an empty beer-glass. "There's a voluptuousness in dolor; know, my dear, that one loves dolor.

"You don't believe me, child? Because, devoid of will and devoid of thought, I stroll through life like someone half-asleep, you tell yourself that no emotion has ever caused my nerves to vibrate? When I was young—for I have been young, young man!—I was, like you who are listening to me, avid for sensation. I said to myself: 'Too bad if sensation kills me!' I remember . . . and it seems to me also that I am as if I had been killed.

"Is it possible that at twenty, I wrote verses, and I believed something, and I thought? So, I, who am talking to you, was a poet, and convinced, as no one any longer is today, and I was curious for enjoyment. Any emotion gives an enjoyment, no matter whether it is sweet or bitter; it doesn't matter; everything that is emotion

---

[1] Joris-Karl Huysmans (1848-1907) was a regular contributor to the *Revue Independante*, which serialized his novel *En Rade* (1886-87; book 1887).

creates enjoyment, and I was in quest of emotions. So, I said to myself, at first: one enjoys everything that is a sensation. But soon I said to myself: banal, insignificant and infantile is the pleasure that is born of contentment; happiness is a paltry agent of sensuality; one doesn't feel a mild sensation; strong joy is only obtained by the harshness of sensation. Then, by virtue of a refined curiosity of enjoyment, I wanted crises of the flesh and the spirit. In the same way that a drunkard only wants alcohol that burns his throat, I only wanted an anguish to tear my heart; I enjoyed the contemplation of my dolors as others enjoy the consciousness of their serenity. And I was no longer satisfied by the emotions that circumstances brought me, I wanted to provoke them; I tortured myself—for the pleasure.

"At twenty, I abandoned religion, to which I had given myself recklessly, because, after having disturbed my adolescence with its mystical fever, it no longer acted reliably on my rational youth; and I demanded its anguishes from amour. Would you like to know how, once among many other times, I rendered myself miserable in order to enjoy it? Listen to this story, my lad, and profit from it, if it pleases you.

"At twenty-three—unless it was sooner, or later—having already had a few romantic passions, I saw a woman I desired. I've forgotten her name, and what she did, and what she looked like . . . in sum, I really wanted her. I told myself that I ought to love her; for a fortnight—having never spoken to her, you'll divine—I occupied myself with giving myself that amour; I intoxicated myself with words; I proved to myself that she was sovereignly beautiful and lovable; and consciously, I affirmed to myself that I loved her . . .

"What a joy it is to love, to have one's heart gripped by raw desire, one's senses on fire, one's mind obsessed by an image, a continuous fever! After a fortnight, I ought to have been quite content with myself, having put myself in a suitable state of overexcitement, I began to be persuaded that I loved that woman; by dint of telling myself that I loved her, I believed it; by dint of wanting to love her, I loved her. From then on, not having her, I became unhappy; and, in the extreme depths of my being, I saluted the bitter emotion.

"It was necessary, therefore, to think about approaching her. I resolved to do everything in order to have her. She was almost unapproachable for me; I believe now, that she was a woman of the theater. I didn't have a sou, I was ugly and I was stupid. As soon as I had thought of going to find her, I was gripped by fear; another fortnight passed thus. My passion heated up; the difficulty was a stimulant. In any case, imagination worked hard; I no longer had any other idea; desire maddened me, and I was consumed by my impotence.

"Oh, the sufferings of unsatisfied passion, of desire, of the fever of vain desire! The enjoyments!

"Does that astonish you, child? You don't think . . .

"It's because, you see, fortunate amour, the amour that is a repose, doesn't give strong emotion, and if it still fills the heart, it doesn't agitate it; fortunate amour doesn't cause suffering. When one believes oneself to be an artist, one has the right to be original. I wanted emotions, damn it! I'd have them; I'd throw myself in the fire in order to be warm; in order not to be troubled by a light I'd have put out my eyes. That time, I was in search of an unhappy amour.

"I spoke to that woman. Prepared as I was, from the first conversation I was intoxicated; the amour that I wanted to have, I had; it didn't matter how that amour was born; now, it existed; I was in love. She didn't reject me. I did crazy things; I think I borrowed money and spent it on gifts; she esteemed me then, a demonstrative fellow, and showed herself increasingly gracious; I even seemed to perceive, after some time, a benevolent sentiment. I hadn't hoped for so much felicity; my passion took a pleasant road; I let myself go; gradually, I followed the slope of my fortunate amour; I glimpsed imminent delights; that damnable imagination built paradises, and I saw them rising, all in blue and gold; I entered the land of happiness . . .

"That was what I couldn't support for long. In happiness there's scarcely any enjoyment; one only enjoys, greatly, suffering. The reproduction of beings, that voluptuousness, is the supreme suffering of the individual; it exhausts and it kills, reproducing; in the kiss, there is the sob, the spasm and the swoon, and the ruination of bodies, and the collapse of minds; and that is the great enjoyment.

"Finally, one evening, I had a rendezvous. I swear to you that I loved that woman then, in all my thought and my flesh; I would have got myself killed for her; I would have liked to die in the intoxication of her kiss. Well, having tortured myself for that first rendezvous, having wanted it for a month amid the mortal frisson of passion, that first amorous rendezvous, coldly, of my own free will, deliberately, without excusing myself, I missed it; and that evening, while she was waiting for me with smiles. I, in order to know that anguish, stayed at home, pale, looking at my watch, at the adorable and blissful hour of the kiss passing by—the monstrous hour in which I organized my own torture.

"Two days later, I went back, broken-hearted, imploring forgiveness; I was sent away.

"You will say that it was my own fault; that my misfortune was merited; that I'm unworthy of any pity; assuredly, you don't feel sorry for me.

"Oh, I was unhappy! For several weeks I couldn't even speak to her. And at night, I sobbed, I called out to her; I writhed in the fury of my solitude. One evening, after days of dry despair, I wept for two hours, like a baby. She occupied my existence. As in novels, I no longer ate, I slept badly, and I went pale. Do you know what it feels like to have frantic and unsatisfied desires and bleak sorrows in which thought drowns, and the stupor of ultimate malaise? In sum, it's the extreme of misery, to know oneself to be culpable and to curse one's unique enemy, one's torturer . . . well, those sobs, those fevers, those cries, those tears and those rages against oneself— the suffering—it's the flesh in which joy exists.

Those, my young friend, were my best days; they were the ones when I was most alive. I was in love and I was suffering. I had wanted to love a woman; I had loved her; I had fled her arms; I had returned; I had been rejected. Later, she took pity . . . I no longer recall what happened. She was beautiful; she had a smile in which my soul took flight; her breast was as soft as her breath . . . I think I was her lover . . .

"Oh, the suffering of desperate days! All my youth, I lived the thrice intense life of dolor. I was young, I was a poet, I was convinced.

"You see, my friend, I lived so much, at that age, that today, it's finished; I am, believe me, heart-broken, my body worn out, and my soul burned. Now, nothing much remains to me. But what a joyful time there was!

"Love dolor, my son. It's the supreme enjoyment."

THE CABALIST

IT is a pleasant thing to be tranquil in one's illusion. I am very calm, very good and quite inoffensive, and so accommodating that my brother has kept me, an old bachelor, in the midst of his family. No evil thought occurs to me; I don't inconvenience anyone; I'm placid and content with everything, and in the armchair where I spend my days, it's as if I weren't there. That's because I don't live in the same world as you; I have my own universe, more beautiful than yours.

Once, I recall, when I was a reasonable man, like all men, I had gradually observed—a sad experience—that there is no true human happiness, that everything escapes humans and deceives them—O unslakable desire! I said then that this world is bad and that I wanted to live in another.

In another world I live. I've learned how that is possible; to go away from the earth, enter a new country, to live there, to march in a region of dream, to live with phantoms, to be the guest of a realm of fays, and lodge in palaces of immaterial gold and imponderable pearls. I worked very hard to acquire that science, and I acquired it; the veils of knowledge fell away, I discovered worlds other than the human world and by what means the empires that humans do not see can be conquered.

I learned that everything is an emanation of one eternal and infinite Substance, absolute Being, formless and nameless; terrestrial human being is the image of celestial human being, and the universes are reflections of Unity; universes are the forms of Substance; there are appearances. But the appearance that we see is not the only one; there is an infinite number of others, an infinite number of universes that we don't know, and which, similarly, are deceptive manifestations of the Infinite, vain forms of the Absolute, illusory emanations of Being. That is the information of the Sepher Yetzirah, as well as the Zohar.

Among that infinity of worlds, outside the world visible to humans, I searched for a world of my own. I found one. I found, very close to your world, a superior world, where I live.

I've learned that around us, subtle creatures exist, essences of matter, composed of imperceptible atoms, pure principles of elements; we call them Spirits but, as I said, they are only extremely fine matter. They live in the earth's orbit, and can be conjured by humans; then they become sensible and visible to them; some are fiery, which are called Salamanders; others are airy, Sylphes; Gnomes, the guardians of treasure, are earthen, and the last, Undines, watery; they have human faces; they live like humans, and there are males and females; they're benevolent, helpful and gracious, obedient and faithful, but it's necessary to conjure them.

Solomon conjured them, Esdras and Elia; the rabbis Akiva and Simon ben Jochai, who wrote about the art; Pythagoras, Plato and Philo knew them, and Valentinus the Heresiarch, Avicenna, the physician of Caliphs, and Paracelsus; the Comte de Gabalis gave his name to the work, as Pico della Mirandola reports, Raymond Lull the revelator, Johannes Reuchlin, Guillaume Postel and many others; Orpheus, Robert Fludd and van Helmont have testified to their spiritual commerce.

In order to see Spirits, converse with them and command them, it's necessary to learn the secret of evocation. What is it? Know that it is necessary to appropriate the essence of each of the four elements, the fire of the Sun in the form of imponderable powder, the substance of water, that of the earth and a drop of pure air; when you possess the talisman, you can renounce the human world. Know that that alone is difficult; that is the entire proof; magical science is accessible; the practice of the talisman is easy; but it's necessary to detach oneself from humanity; it's necessary to prefer that world to this one; it's necessary to say: I want. It's necessary to want; the will is everything; in truth, will is sufficient.

All the worlds are, in fact, only representations, appearances, illusions; nothing exists except for absolute Unity; worlds are phantasmagorias. The world of spirits is neither more nor less real than the human world; it's a form, an emanation; like the others, it's a mobile shadow; all worlds are made of thought. Whatever the world might be that thought conceives, you can live there if your soul takes refuge there; the world of spirits is a chimerical world that my thought has created; it exists in my thought; it therefore exists, like the human world, if my soul flies there; I tell you that in order to live here, it's sufficient to want to live there.

Personally, I wanted that. When you see me remaining motionless for long hours, as mute as if in sleep, it's because I'm conversing, internally, with gnomes or goblins; and when I smile, silently, in the large armchair where you always see me sitting, it's because an undine, ingenuously, is allowing me to see the milky whiteness of her breast, behind a silver rock.

The other evening, I encountered an old Trilby—that's a sylph[1]—in an aerial park sanded with ethereal diamonds; he was singing, astride a ray of starlight; I talked to him, and he replied to me, and I asked him to take him with me. "So be it," he said. Then I climbed on to a ray of starlight with the Trilby and we arrived in a country of subtle fire; the lyre-carrying singer, Apollo, was there. I heard his voice, and his lyre; his voice was a concert in which choirs of men, women and children were singing; a polyphony of varied tones radiated from his lyre, infinite nuances of sound that melted into a single mystical sonority.

The other evening, while my relatives had gone to the theater, why did I want to remain in the depths of the obscure drawing room? I could see the proud rocky summits, the forests of fir-trees, the pointed peaks, and

---

1 Charles Nodier's *Trilby out le lutin d'Argail* (1822) was the inspiration of the 1832 ballet *La Sylphide*, with music by Jean-Madeline Schneizhoeffer and choreography by Filippo Taglioni, and for a subsequent ballet produced in 1870, hence the odd character of the reference.

the guardian precipices in which the world lies, the great solemn corteges of the clouds and the desolate vastness of the Valkyrian refuges; and under the lance of the Terrible, the crackling flame sprang forth, ran, swam, flew, the universal fire, to the tintinnabulating explosions of the dancing furies . . .

Oh, Brunhilde, my strong woman, lying asleep in the celestial peace of divine conflagrations—calm, benevolent sleep—Brunhilde, hope for Him: Hero will come, the awakener, Noble will come, vanquisher of gods, superb and regal . . . on the transfulgurant rock, Brunhilde, in the indubitable expectation, sleep, beloved, amid the jubilant flame; I sense you, and I think of you, and in the majestic merry blossoming of fire, with you I dream of future Twilights. O sleeper of divine pasts . . .

Superhuman world, I dwell there! In a superhuman world I live, in the same way that you live in the human world; I really see it; my magical hosts exist; I see them through these eyes; they speak to me and these ears hear them; and I feel them touch me; my eyes, my mouth, my ears, my fingers and my breast all have sensations, and I am happy and calm and utterly inoffensive.

I live in the dream and the illusion. Yes, I know the dream and the illusion; I know the error, I too am conscious of my madness. But I say: blessed is the eye that deceives me, blessed is the ear that lies to me, blessed are the senses by which I am abused! Blessed is my mind, which enables me to see that which has no lines, to touch that which has no substance, and the savor that which has no consistency! Blessed is error!

And if, between two visions, between two hallucinations, as you would say, between two follies—how do I know how many words you have invented, O sages!—if, at times, a reasonable person comes to tell me that it is all lies, I reply: "Well, I knew that . . ." Even during the hallucination I have the sentiment of a hallucination; at the moment when these eyes are seeing the golden palace, I know that, in seeing it, they are deceived; I am conscious of my error, that I am dreaming, and that I am a madman.

But first of all, what does it matter to me, if, in the meantime, I have a hallucination that charms me, if I have a vision, if I have an illusion, if I enjoy it as a reality, and if my dream rises up before my senses and before my mind? And then, I will also reply to you, is not error the universal truth?

Don't laugh at the old cabalist. I am conscious of my error, O humans, and I have accepted it freely; you are unconscious of your error. Humans, your truth is a lie; your world is no more real than mine; your world is a world of illusion; you live in a lie; all of us, you and me, live in illusion, inhabitants of imaginary worlds. Illusions ourselves, beings without existence, forms among the infinity of forms, fleeting emanations of the Unity, pale images of celestial humankind, sad shadows of Adam-Kadmon, who, in the holy Merkabah, is manifested internally by the ten sublime ideal Sephiroths.

I am abused, and so are you; but since everything is appearance, I prefer my madness, which is beautiful; I am happy and good and calm in my dream, whereas you groan in yours; and I praise my fate, considering yours, in the full consciousness of my error, if, veritably, while you are toiling over your false realities, I, a placid and smiling soul, go away under a fay's mantle of clouds to the lands of the Occident, where gentle singing Salamanders dance in a crimson sun, and to the cool dwellings of the dawn, where white virgins, sylphides and undines, who do not exist but whom I can see, surround me with laughter and odorous breath, and form around me, as real to my eyes as the groups of your miseries are to yours, choirs that are a divine grace, and, I know, an illusion.

A TESTAMENT

"IT'S such a long time since we met," he said to me, "that I feared being indiscreet in summoning you to my house this evening; but since you're here and are willing to listen to me, I'll speak to you without reticence and without false modesty: know a human existence."

It was nine o'clock; four candles on the mantelpiece illuminated the narrow and low drawing room, encumbered by ottomans and covered with thick carpets. He was seated in an armchair and I was facing him on a sofa; and I considered that man, still young, of an elegant and aristocratic correction, speaking without moving, without gestures, calmly—and sometimes, half-smiles of distant sorrows died away on his lips.

After a moment of silence, he looked at me and said, very simply: "I desired to talk to you this evening, Monsieur, because tomorrow would have been too late; tonight, I shall kill myself."

I uttered an exclamation and rose to my feet. He made me a sign to sit down again.

"You've promised to listen to me," he continued, "So I'll begin; you shall know the reason for my resolution and you will not dissuade me from it; it's my story that I'm going to tell you."

I sat down and I listened; his words have remained in my memory just as he pronounced them, grave and tranquil.

He said to me: "If you want to know my age, I'm forty years old; I was born in Paris; my father was a former colonel, my mother the child of an old rich family; I had no brother or sister; I did not marry and I had no friends. I spent my adolescence in the tedium of insignificant chatter, at college. When I emerged, I lost my father, and the following year, my mother. At twenty years of age I was alone and free; I did not adopt a profession and tried the life of society; a few months disgusted me with it. Nothing interested me; I did not like anything; nothing pleased me; I did not desire anything; no occupation attracted me and, as need did not force me to take up any, I had none. Pleasure was no more seductive to me than work; lassitude was everywhere.

"I had heard mention of people who were passionate, some for one thing and others for another, but I could not comprehend those passionate individuals. What was the point of activity? Why frequent people when one can live alone? Why act when repose is permitted? All that appeared good to me was isolation and idleness: to ignore others and to be ignored by them; not to act, not to reflect, and to try to forget that one exists. Thus, I scorned what others love, happy only in sensing my individuality dissolving in indolence. And I wondered—the only question I asked myself—why other men acted, and how it could be that anyone was interested in life.

"I did not esteem life at all; I retrenched myself from it, and wanted to enjoy placidity. In the fullness of youth, I made myself an existence of solitude, calm, and sloth. Travel has a thousand disagreements for one dubious pleasure; I detested it, and remained in Paris. The installation of my apartment was my principal preoccupation; everything was disposed for the comfort of idleness; my domestic carried out my undemanding orders silently; and I spent the time thus: I got up late, time spent in bed being, perhaps, the best part of existence; in the morning, some excursion on foot or on horseback; I had lunch at home, alone, and when the meal was over I sat for an hour or two in an armchair; I went away with my cigar smoke into the blue and white. Before dusk, a second excursion, a banal stroll along the boulevards; there is a charm in considering the swarming crowd, busy or annoyed, unknown to it, and traversing it without mingling with it; from a table in a café, smoking—in order to put a cloud between the world and me—I took pleasure in seeing the vague flock of passers-by: a secret delight in contemplating, through a window, a tempest outside. Then dinner, and the solitary evening, with the reverie of the fireside in winter, the open window in summer, or with the amusement of some book, I interrupted my object-free meditations. And while strolling. I heard confusedly, around me, the living rumors of the crowd, to which my voice did not add.

"I was not born to be a man of the Occident—but are Oriental tales more lies?—only envying drinkers of opium and eaters of hashish; I would have liked to lose myself thus in the infinite scintillation of the sky, where

89

thought gradually dissipates and the self evaporates. But human passions were despicable inanities; I never believed in religion, the mad imaginations of the desperate avid for life; I never believed in amour; there is only self-love, and what is called amour is the supreme egotism . . . Perhaps it is a pleasure to become gradually drowsy in a conscious dream, on the bosom of a beautiful woman, and to lose, in the caresses of perfumed female hair, the sentiment of the world and oneself: the pleasure of a small boy, the sickening of which comes before the teeth of reason.

"The only thing that is good is not to be.

"So, I lived in sovereign detachment from humankind; I delivered myself, body and soul, to contemplative indolence; and I did not understand how other people interested themselves in things; it seemed to me to be an inexplicable enigma that, things being so despicable, people were so avid for things. Gradually, the question became insistent before me; it solicited me; it pursued me, pressed me and harassed me; it was necessary to respond to it . . .

"Oh, the misery of being human! Why, if one aspires to inaction, can one not put the mind to sleep and close it to thought, and give it the calm of brutishness? Or, if such a sacrifice is impossible, why can one not fortify one's mind with activity, robust thought and healthy toil? But for whoever has opted for idleness and scorn of life, dreads, if the mind has remained capable of an idea, if it has not become inapt for reflection and its not brutalized; for in the midst of its idleness, the chimera will come to plant itself there, and no one will be able to sever its invasive roots.

"Personally, I had gradually been caught by the question of the why and how of existence. During the leisure of my idleness, my thought, emptied of the realities of that existence, went fatally to the dreams of its anxiety. Having passed through the world without finding anything there but ennui and disgust, believing in neither religion nor amour, having nothing at heart but scorn for all human activity, I contemplated surrounding things silently, at random, and told myself incessantly that the cause was not apparent. I thought about the lives of human beings, the passionate and the indolent, and I told myself that all that was not easily explicable, and, having retired entirely to the calm of my comfort, I could not help interrogating myself anxiously, about the reason for what I scorned and fled.

"It was then that the chimera rose up in my mind: it seemed to me that the human world was no longer sufficient to itself: an absurd, illogical, incoherent world, ruled by vanity, a risible and pitiful sequence of phenomena in which the contradictory was engendered, where effects did not respond to causes, as if a mysterious and very powerful force were turning this way and that.

"The object of my confused meditations, amid the idleness of my days and the insomnia of my days, that astonishment at finding the world such was born of my disdain for humankind; that astonishment had provoked the need for an explanation; the explanation was the chimera that came to seize my mind and went to wrap it in an idea.

"Gradually, I persuaded myself that the cause was extranatural; the thought came to me that things, being absurd and contradictory, had a reason for being outside themselves: that the visible and the tangible had for a complement the invisible and the intangible; that the material universe supposed another universe; that the natural world was supported, necessarily, upon a supernatural world. But what was that unknown?

"By virtue of laxity of temperament, habitual sloth, mental indolence, I declined in scrutinizing that question; lying in an armchair, wandering solitary in a desert or a populous promenade, I turned the problem over and over, like a child with a coconut that he does not know how to open. A detestable existence; either it was necessary to live, like others, in passion and life, or it was necessary to forget everything that was life, but I was condemned not to live, and yet to suffer life . . .

"At the present moment, on the point of ending it, I judge myself and I say: the misfortune is when the mind, accustomed to idleness, falls prey to the chimera, and, in order to struggle against its harassments, has not been nourished on the green pasture of reality.

"I too, disdainful of human misery, had been gripped by human misery by virtue of that idea: that there is, perhaps, outside this natural world, something supernatural; and, always seeming fully impassive, I suffered more than the others from the human malaise, the eternal anxiety of thought. There was, above me, something supernatural, and I wondered what it was, that terrible, unfathomable thing. The idea possessed me, and my mind was like a dilapidated castle where ungraspable phantoms wandered constantly, never dissipated.

"One evening, at the end of winter, after many days and many nights of futile meditations—I had only gone out for an hour in the morning, and all afternoon I had remained near the fire, in the mild warmth of my room, reading, dreaming and smoking, while the indifferent hours flowed by—my domestic had served me dinner. Then, as night was approaching, without light, numbed by the moist warmth of the large wood fire that was crackling in the hearth, I became drowsy momentarily. When I awoke, after half an hour, the obscurity had increased; from the firmly closed windows an increasingly somber light was falling with the reflection of the streetlamps, and in the upholstered chamber the silhouette of the furniture was vague, glimpsed by the glow of the wood fire.

"To begin with, like any sleeper who wakes up, it took me a second or two to recover my senses; I don't know what dream had occupied my short slumber; having passed my hand over my eyes and chased away the last mists of drowsiness, I resumed, in the near-darkness, the full cognizance of things and sat up in my armchair.

"Then—was it the consequence of my long anxious reveries or my fears?—I had a sensation: a sensation of something spiritual, absolutely unknown and mysterious, like the one that obsessed me. It was as if a spirit were there: a spirit, a thought, a soul . . . the perception was instantaneous; There was, present, intangible and invisible, but there, a soul that was not my soul, a thought above my thought; it was something indefinite, but very real, and which weighed upon me intellectually, as if the spiritual world were colliding with my spirit; I sensed a thought, and I could not comprehend what the thought was, but it was the impact of another, indefinable mind; and I had the sentiment of a manifestation, before my soul, of a world.

"Stupor seized me; confused interrogations rolled through my brain; and what struck me above all was that I must have had the obscure sensation of something supernatural.

"O thought of the supernatural! Obsession with the thought of the supernatural! Mysterious obsession, by which the mind is relentlessly persecuted, and which nothing human can vanquish, since it is the obsession of the supernatural!

"I once knew a man who believed in the existence of a fantastic world, which he wanted to invoke; thirty years of spiritual tension gave him the devastating hallucination of the phantom. Later, meditating on my adventure, I thought about that man and I compared myself, me, the idle dreamer, with him, the laborious toiler, both haunted by a supernatural idea, unexplained, somber and terrible for me, reflective and clear to him; and I considered his end and mine, and I envy him, who went away with the possession of his dream, while I am dying of the incomprehensibility of mine.

"Thus, the scorn and disgust for humankind, the mania of an explanation, and the obsession of that absurd, irremediably obscure explanation, the supernatural, haunts me, and sometimes I believe I see in my mind vague terrifying visions of the fantastic thing that is floating above me.

"Life, with that anguish, could not be borne; I wanted to tame the accursed idea; I excited my will against my mind. Alas, in idleness and indolence, I had even enervated my will. A worthy result. To the torment of the first obsession another was added, effort, and I did not chase the enemy away. I tried other distractions; I lived in society, I went to fêtes, I sought pleasure, I strove to love; I constrained myself thus to an odious existence, but I could not efface from my mind what I wanted to efface. Sometimes, in the momentum of an orgy, I forgot; then, as soon as I was alone and immobile, the chimera reappeared. I tried not to be alone and immobile any longer; I exaggerated the impetus of my dissipation, and I ran madly from one excitement to another; no, I could not eradicate the ineradicable.

"And because I was haunted by an idea, I lived—me, the enjoyer of quietude—in a fever of activity. I traveled; traveling bored me; I walked for weeks, but on the roads and in the mountains I had phantasmagorical sensations that made me go pale. I even attempted work . . .

"And among the studies, during the perilous excursions in the mountains, the promenades in joyous company, the suppers at which I got drunk, in the arms of my mistresses, I said to myself, secretly, that something mysterious and supernatural existed; suddenly, it seemed to me that I was about to sense, against my soul, a thought, a spirit, like the manifestation of something vague; and it seemed to me that I sensed the soul, the thought, the spirit, the vague thing.

"Then, since I was too weak, and the idea could not be vanquished, what was the point of fatiguing myself further with a hateful existence? Better to resign myself! I abandoned social life, pleasures and distractions, for the second time, I returned to the idle calm of before, and I found myself once again, alone, in the dreamy indolence of my old life, face to face with my torture.

"Don't seek any other cause for the death that I'm giving myself; I can't reject, and don't want to bear, the torture of my obsession. In my idleness, an idea has taken root, and all my thoughts are entangled with it. I have disdained human passions, and the activity of which objects are the vanity, and pleasures, and life; but outside of all human passion, all activity, all end of pleasure, and outside all reality—is it a mysterious punishment?—an extrahuman idea has seized my mind; an invincible monster is lodged in my brain, and is deranging it with its visions. Oh, something supernatural . . . is there a supernatural? There is, for it envelops and is crushing my thought; there is, but what is it? What would the mind see if it could see? All around my soul there are, vaguely, unknown souls; the world is full of invisible and imponderable phantoms; their breath traverses my thought, tenebrously, and in my soul, I sense them. I cannot say that there is not something supernatural.

"So, I am renouncing despicable and dolorous life. Woe betide the man whose unoccupied mind is haunted by the chimera . . .

"That is my story, Monsieur; you will know tomorrow why I am dead, and you can say so, if you wish."

HELL

ONE day, I went to see a man who is my friend and my adviser, Doctor Daniel D***, a physician forty-five or forty-six years old, a grave intelligence, known for his work in scientific philosophy. I found him in his small drawing room, holding a book.

"This," he said, "is a book somewhat out of place in the hands of a physician and an unbeliever; it's Pascal's *Pensées*."

Sitting in a low armchair, leaning his chin on one of his hands, looking at me with his large profound eyes, Daniel D*** spoke without a crease troubling the calm of his very broad and square forehead, already bald, bordered by black hair. Daniel D*** was tall and vigorous; his head was forceful, his face clean-shaven and pale; sometimes, in considering him, I thought of the portraits one sees of Edgar Poe.

Dusk was approaching; the light from outside struck his brown-haired head fully, in the depths of the darkening room; "This Pascal," he said to me, "I don't have his beliefs, but he astonishes me. For example, the chapter of the wager, which I can refute with a word, it troubles me."

I pressed my friend on that subject, and he went on.

"To be religious or not to be religious; that is the whole question for Pascal. Philosophically, Pascal is a skeptic; according to Pascal, reason cannot establish anything; reason cannot indicate any truth to us; the religious question is, rationally, insoluble. Practically, however, it is necessary to decide, to know which way to turn, to choose one's path. Thus in the uncertainty of our reason, when it is a matter of living, should we opt for religion, or against religion? That is the special object of the chapter called the Wager."

"And the doctor read these lines:

"*Let us examine this point, therefore, and let us say: Either God exists, or he does not. But to which side should we incline? Reason cannot determine anything in the matter; there is an infinite chaos that separates us. A game is played, at the extremity of that infinite distance where it will turn up heads or tails. Which do you choose? By reason you cannot decide one or the other; by reason you cannot defend either one . . ."*

Doctor D*** continued commentating on the continuation of the text of the *Pensées*: "Let our interest inform us, therefore. It's a wager that is proposed to us, a bet; when one cannot choose certainly; it's necessary to gamble; but let us gamble sagely, let us see where and interest is more extensive. Let us examine this point, therefore, and let us say: either God exists, or he does not. If you bet on the existence of God, then if God exists, you gain everything, and if he does not exist, you have not lost anything. But if you bet against, you still lose nothing if he does not exist, but if he does exist, you lose everything. The choice is therefore evident. Bet heads, that God exists. Now, as a God, however he is conceived, is the principle of all religions, bet heads for religion, and follow your wager to the end. The ascetic Jansenism of Pascal is a rigorously logical Christianity, so bet, according to Pascal, on God, the Fall, and Grace.

"A single word ruins that reasoning; one bets, in fact, only if one is in doubt; people who are assuredly incredulous, not being in doubt, have no need to bet. One can refuse the alternative of the wager. Thus, the whole edifice of logic is destroyed. And yet, how powerful the doctrine of Pascal is!"

Doctor Daniel D*** talked about other things. I came to read him some of these stories of demonomania, possession and the Cabala. He listened to me, making particular observations after each story. When I had finished and he had made his final remarks, after a moment of silence, he raised his head slowly, leaned back in his armchair, and then he spoke.

※

"Stories of demonomania, possession and the Cabala," he said to me, "have become implausible. Today, the supernatural is far from us; the preoccupation with the supernatural is no longer in minds; we can no longer conceive of men obsessed by ideas of magic, sorcery and demonology; the occult sciences are no longer interesting; the fantastic has had its time; the supernatural is fading away; we cannot believe that there are still humans tormented by the supernatural."

I made a few objections.

He continued: "You know my opinions, my young friend, so I shall talk without any reticence. You know that I'm an atheist and a materialist; I don't hide it, nor do I glory in it, and I intend, especially with you, to speak freely, in accordance with my conscience.

"The supernatural is being forgotten; religions are paling; theologies are disappearing; in the human mind there is no longer room for any but natural ideas. All of human history can, in fact, be summarized in two words: Magic and Science. Since human beings have existed, those two words, Magic and Science, can serve to express the development of humankind: humankind has only been progressing from one toward the other; having departed from Magic, it has headed toward Science.

"The first animals that were human, considering the spectacle of nature scattered all around them, must have been seized by an immense fearful astonishment; seeing rivers flow, seas swell, trees grow, go green and yellow and green again, periodically, tempests rumbling, with avalanches and darkness, the sun born in the orient rising into the heavens and descending again, obscure night and the evolutions of the stars, and meteors, and the infinite metamorphoses of existences, and finding themselves engulfed therein, feeble beings impotent to change anything; they wondered, did they not, what caused those rivers to flow, those seas to swell, why those tempests, why the daylight, why the night, and why all those monstrous phenomena whose agents were not apparent? The eternal question; the human mind is such that the explanation of things is a need for it; and, then as now, indefinitely, the same interrogation haunts the human mind.

"Well, to that interrogation, two responses are possible: one alleges that the phenomena of nature are, universally, produced by fixed laws, the necessary relationships of things; the other alleges that they are ordered by free hidden wills that are revealing their action. The first only discovers nature in nature; the second divines behind its veil something exterior that commands; one declares that everything is inevitable, the other that everything is the accidental effect of capricious causes. I call all supernatural religion Magic—I say Magic, not Magism; a magician is not a mage.

"A human being will accept one of the two explanations; in order for him to accept the first, it is necessary that he has observed some natural laws; he will conclude that phenomena are mechanical if he has known the organization of a machine. But for someone who knows nothing among the infinity of things, only the other response is intelligible; primitive humans gazing, bewildered, across the abyss of the universe, in the confusion of appearances, must necessarily have thought that everything visible was a manifestation, either of very numerous invisible spirits, or of one omnipotent invisible spirit, but assuredly of a mysterious force acting sovereignly upon nature.

"That is why the human being who believes in certain essential laws will seek to discover those laws, to make use of them, and to constrain nature naturally. On the contrary, the other wants to attain, not the phenomenon, but the supernatural agent of the phenomenon, and by means of prayers of conjurations, he expects his desire to be granted by the agent, the cause, the motor, the commander, the god. Now, the former is the work of the scientist, the latter the work of the magician; the one is Magic and the other Science.

"Thus, ancient humans, not yet being scientists, were magicians. From theoretical magic, practical magic emerges: belief in spirits, in gods, in Providence, in creation, polytheism and monotheism, theurgy and deism; all of that, which confesses something exterior to nature, is magical faith; conjurations, exorcisms, evocations, sacrifices, rites, implorations, all kneeling and all prayer is practical magic, wanting a natural effect to descend from a supernatural cause. Different from one another in their figures, all religions and all theist philosophers have the same blood in their bodies; they belong to the Magical race; their last scion you have named: when occult beliefs are forgotten and religion dies, the obsession with the supernatural in the mind will vegetate too, a vague phantom, an insubstantial shadow, an extreme incarnation of antique expired Magic. The obsession of the supernatural, known to be false, is the last residue of Magic.

"Magic was the commencement of everything; humankind's first books were books of magic; religions are magic; the ancient philosophers were magicians disdainful of practical magic, avid for a magical explanation of the universe; Christianity proclaimed the dogma of Providence, by which the supernatural is mingled with every instant of natural phenomena; in the meantime, humans demand from divine simulacra rain, fine weather and a large number of children. The shadow of magic envelops the world.

"Gradually, however, very slowly, like the first light of dawn appearing in the vastness of darkness, the constancy of natural laws gleamed; unity became manifest within diversities, fatality among accidents; things were illuminated, nature whitened with the dawn, the principle of Science emerged over the horizon, within the floods of Magic. Then, after Agrippa and the scholar-magicians, came Kepler and modern scientists; Magic, expelled from the heavens, expelled from the earth, expelled from animality, took refuge in the intellectual; the last debris of theological doctrines were spiritualism and spiritism, an unacknowledged child; but Science has pursued Magic everywhere; it has come and it has said: human mind, you are only a function of the brain; human soul, you are only the name of physiological life. Science rose into the sky and its splendor became radiant, for the sun rose, resplendent, celestially beautiful, toward the zenith, while Magic plunged toward the nadir.

"Magic—which is to say, religious philosophy, the spiritualist doctrine, belief in the Creator and faith in Providence—has disappeared; Science has made God an unnecessary hypothesis; there is no supernatural, there is no motor, no first principle, no God; there is only eternal, living nature. Nature is life. Who has given movement and force to things? Matter is essentially mobile and strong; it is life. There is no supernatural; I tell you that there is nothing but eternal living nature.

"So, no more superstitions, no more religious dreads, no more supernatural anguish; belief in the supernatural has become a historical fact. No more thought of the supernatural, no more of that old residue of primitive ignorance; our real miseries are quite enough; the chimera is flying away; we see clearly before us; the supernatural is exiting the human mind."

Doctor Daniel D*** having finished that speech, after a few moments, I replied.

"I won't dispute your opinions; that isn't my concern. I admire your natural philosophy but I have a tenderness for the beautiful figures of mythology. I don't pride myself on wisdom; science and religions, magism and magic, are dear to me. I loved Lucretius and I loved Virgil. I can be a believer with *Port-Royal* and an atheist with Büchner,[1] in all religions and all philosophies with our eternal master, poetry. In any case, permit me not to defend the things in my tales; but tell me: because Magic will pass, will all trace of Magic be effaced from souls? A memory remains of an abolished belief; do you believe that, because the ideal of the supernatural will no longer exist, the supernatural will be dead, buried and forgotten? Do you not know anyone before whom it has reappeared? Have even you, my dear scientist, never glimpsed the shadow of the dead? Has your materialistic

---

[1] *Port-Royal* (1837-59) is Charles Augustin Sainte-Beuve's history of a Jansenist abbey. The German philosopher Ludwig Büchner (1824-1899) was a leading exponent of scientific naturalism, but the speaker might also be thinking of his brother Georg (1813-1837), whose play *Dantons Tod* (1835; tr. as *Danton's Death*) includes a famous nihilistic fable.

and atheist faith never been tempted? Oh, it would only be an effect of heredity, a debris of old humanity, an insignificant weakness . . . but have you never known that weakness? Has no thought of the supernatural ever troubled, if only for a second, involuntarily, the limpid calm of your brain?"

"I've told you," the physician replied, "that I refuse the alternative of Pascal's wager. I have no uncertainty; I am assured in my atheism; I have no doubt; I do not want to wager."

"There are assured men, then! Are the incredulous saved from doubt, better than the saints and martyrs? Is doubt not the eternal torture? Pascal was a Christian obsessed by doubt; are the atheists of today not tormented by it? Can anyone affirm the stability of his belief? The religious have groaned because of the anguish of doubt; will strong minds say that the thought has never come to them: but what if there is a God?"

The doctor was silent. I went on.

"It seems to me that doubt is the eternal torture. The religious believe in the existence of God; atheists believe in the non-existence of God; they believe similarly; they have their faith. But to all of them, the uncertainty comes: what if there is no God? what if there is? An absence of God for the religious; an existence for the atheists: similarly, it is the implausible imagined to be true. It is the monstrous chance of loss: the lightning might strike at a million points, one of which is your head; thus, one chance of being hit against a million chances of not being hit, but a chance. Religion is absurd, it is false, it is impossible; but what if that absurdity, that lie, that impossibility, turned out to be . . . A sad, inevitable meditation. Doubt is the old wound, secret and shameful, that gnaws souls eternally religious souls are afflicted, and incredulous souls; it is necessary that the hereditary ulcer germinates and flowers in all human blood."

"Doubt," murmured Daniel D***. "To know that one possesses the truth, and yet to doubt . . ."

"Doubt; and in the meantime, to make a decision, for it is necessary to make a decision. You have made a decision; you have wagered, for it is necessary to wager; you have not wagered on God, you have wagered on no-God, for the wager is an absolute necessity; whoever is not with me is against me. You, assured mind, firm and strong, who have wagered your life, tails, against the supernatural, punter on eternity, beware of the continuation of your life. What if that stupidity were a monstrous reality, what if there were a terrible afterlife beyond death . . . beware of that, and like Wotan, the father of Valhalla, think, god as you are, in anguish and tremulousness."

The evening was increasingly somber; the room was darkening gradually; and in the demi-shadow, I could no longer see anything but the broad, square, bald cranium of my friend, with his two eyes profoundly sunken beneath their eyebrows.

Doctor Daniel D*** did not reply. I looked at him admiringly.

"So," I said, "there is a man who does not protest the word of human weakness; a thinker who does not deny that thought has fears; a bold man who will perhaps confess to me that there are days when he has flinched . . . This man of proven incredulity, of superb atheism, of perfect denial of the supernatural, this assured individual, is wondering, at this moment, whether an anxious thought might not have insinuated itself occasionally into his certainty, and whether he too might have had a disturbance of his confidence, a hesitation, a frisson of supernatural deceptions . . ."

As I was reflecting thus, the physician raised his head, and said to me slowly, almost in a whisper:

"Your words have recalled a very ancient scene to my memory; I want to tell you about it; it is already twenty years old. It's a matter of someone you didn't know, being too young. He was an advocate, a litterateur-philosopher, who won the modest and solid glory of an honest man and a serious thinker.

"The story of his life is banal; it's his death that I want to relate to you, but I have to tell you about his life first.

"When he qualified as an advocate, his small patrimonial fortune was sufficient for him; he did not practice. He occupied himself with literature and published his works, which had some success. His life was orderly. His physiognomy was open and, with some severity, benevolent; his attire was simple, of a correct elegance; since his youth he had been remarked for the meditative air of his features; there was something of the socialite in him and something of the dreamer. Later, he turned toward philosophy; he was a freethinker; he studied political economics; he had a tendency to philanthropy and his colleagues sometimes mocked him, but the mockery was anodyne against his sincerity.

"One day, it was learned that he had bought a villa in the environs of Paris; there he lived for the rest of his life; he got married, and devoted himself entirely to literature, philosophy and his happiness; and that man, who was irreligious and assured, had his reasoned and simple incredulity, unaware of doubt.

"I knew that man during the last four or five years of his life. I was at the beginning of mine. He was a close friend of my father, and I often went to his home, to his villa. Then we talked, I in the impetuosity of my youthful enthusiasms, he calm and grave; the impression has not been effaced in me of his speech and his appearance. Around him there was a comforting air of serenity; one respired peace, strength and wellbeing. His wife had an almost respectful adoration for him, and she was loved. In society he was more than esteemed, he was honored.

"His literary career was not splendid but it was fine; his influence was great and it was good; the man had a righteous mind and his honesty was a strength; even the religious respected the tranquil sincerity of his atheism, as unshakable as a faith. At fifty, going gray, his face was radiant and full of health, with the hint of engaging familiarity that age gives; he received in his villa some of the most considered people in the literary and scientific world; a beautiful life unfurled; the man was happy, because he had fortune, esteem, honors, amity and repose—and also peace of mind. I knew him well; sometimes I stayed with him. I saw him act and think, and I observed his actions and his thoughts; I surprised him in his meditations, interrupted him in his dreams, awoke him from his slumber; I encountered him alone, with his friends, in society and in public; he wanted to call me his physician, and I knew his organism as well as his mind.

"That man was happy; serenity was in his being, like a healthy perfume. He died of a disease of the heart, but, sensing that he was going to die, he rejoiced in departing before the age of infirmities, between his wife and his friends, seeing sincere tears flow; and placidly, he awaited the moment of entering into annihilation. That man, absolutely irreligious, absolutely tranquil, had not been able to wager, never having doubted.

"That was the man that I saw die . . . I was a young man . . . it was twenty years ago . . . I saw the great atheist pass away.

"His death was mild. He was lying in the large low bed, pale and sad, in the middle of the room; the curtains, partially drawn, allowed the summer light to penetrate, attenuated: not a chamber of death but a chamber of repose. His testament was finished; his friends were assembled in a neighboring room; a great silence extended, solemn but not lugubrious; death was approaching slowly—yes, he could see it, without dread; I can affirm that. Of the Christians who were there, none dared name God to that dying man. My master, his old physician and his old friend, was watching at his side; I was standing up, a little further away, considering him. He had not lost consciousness, but he was weakening; his eyes were extinguishing; his head was tilting to the right on the pillow."

Doctor Daniel D*** was speaking very gravely; his gaze was lowered. He fell silent. At that moment, the obscurity was almost complete. A domestic came in, carrying a lamp, which he deposited on a table, and went out. The doctor got up and went to lean against the marble mantelpiece, pensively. Then he raised his pale, square brow, and he said:

"It's strange how that old memory has struck my mind. One might think it a dream that awakening did not dissipate . . . a dream that had recurred several times in twenty years.

"At the instant when his head slid gently over the pillow, I saw his extinct eyes open; his hands clenched slightly, and while his face was inclined toward the sheets, his eyes, which I had seen open, blanched: they were staring, fixedly, straight ahead. I had taken two steps forward and I was before him, leaning over, looking into his face. I saw his lips stir; a green tint passed over his skin, and I thought I heard a word in his mouth . . . but I'm not sure of having heard it . . . his lips had remained open, his eyes gaping and blank. He died."

"And the word?"

Doctor Daniel D*** replied to me, in a whisper: "I thought it was . . . Hell."

And as I remained in the silence of the demi-obscure room, Doctor Daniel D***, who was standing up, leaning against the mantelpiece, placed both elbows abruptly on the marble and took his temples in his hands; the light of the lamp was reflected in the mirror facing him, with the consequence that I could see clearly, in his broad face, the pallor of his distraught features.

Then, in a low, colorless voice, dully, jerkily and violently, almost grimly, he murmured: "Hell! Hell! Perhaps it was Hell; perhaps he was afraid of Hell . . .

"One day—I was twenty-five—a woman had abandoned me; I wanted to die; that night, in my desolate bed, I dreamed about my suicide; and as I was dreaming about it, I suddenly had that thought . . .

"Hell! The mystical abode of the torture of souls, the mysterious Gehenna, the frightening infinity of Dolors. That dream of Suffering, the Monstrous, the Impossible, and the Unimaginable made real . . . what if that turned up?

"For I have wagered; it is necessary to wager, says Pascal; well, yes, it was necessary to wager heads for God, tails for no God, heads for the eternity of Hell and tails for annihilation; it was necessary to make a decision, to choose, to vote, to engage, to enroll; I tell you, myself, that it is necessary to wager Magic or Science, God or Nature, Eternity or Annihilation . . . nothing or Hell . . .

"A God is absurd, a supernatural absurd, all magic and all religion absurd, and above all, that is absurd: Hell. But what if the absurd is true? There are people who say: *credo quia absurdum*.[1] Heads or tails! The million chances are for tails. But what if heads turns up, in which case Hell? That millionth chance leads to God, and Hell. The Impossible would be.

"Yes, all dreads are effaced; the religions are dead; reason is triumphant, science is resplendent; no illusion, no error; I have before me, present and real, I have, distinctly, clearly, certainly, the truth; I have it between my hands; I have made it myself; it is mine; sure of my strength, I have violated antique Nature and I have held

---

[1] "I believe because it is absurd."

her, naked, in my grasp; I am the master of the universe . . . but something of Magic remains, a debris of dead beliefs. A spore of supernatural obsessions is vegetating in the soul, something of magical fears . . . the idea, which troubled the end of the great theist, of an existence after death, and a damnation. For no incredulity is so firm that it does not have to tremble in thinking of this: with a million chances of winning I have wagered tails against God, but there is the millionth chance of losing, one chance of heads—with Hell."

Having passed his hand over his bald head, the doctor straightened up, shook his head, and said to me in a calm voice:

"Poor children of humankind, inheritors of two hundred religious generations, assure yourselves with your scientific certainties. Like anemia, alcoholism and madness, hereditarily, the idea that grips us, poor sons of Adam, will not let us go so soon."

THE APOSTOLATE

To Agénor Boissier[1]

THE end of April: the damp meadows reflected the brilliance of the air; the crests of hills were turning green; alongside the fresh Norman streams the apple-trees white with blossom, the Lucerne and red clover rose up; in the fields there were confusedly joyful vibrations; and the grass smelled good; the scattered herds of cattle wandered slowly and silently; the children of peasants were playing by the roadside.

In the railways station, Mère Arnaud gazed at her son, who was going away: the Reverend Dominican Father Jean Arnaud, who, emerging from distant seminaries, was going to Paris to preach his first sermon.

Four o'clock chimed; the warmth of the declining sun was gentler. Vaguely, Mère Arnaud, bitterly melancholy, considered the carriage in which the pale and black long head of her beloved only son appeared, amid the still-sparkling brightness of the spring sky.

---

[1] Agénor Boissier, a Genevan millionaire, was one of the patrons of the *Revue Wagnérienne*; when this dedication was penned, Dujardin could not know that Boissier would cause the demise of the periodical when he withdrew his support.

Jean Arnaud was thinking about the first sermon that he was going to preach, and of the apostolate.

And while the train carried him out of the good Norman lands toward Paris, while the illuminated landscape filed before his unseeing eyes, motionless in the black pleats of his Dominican mantle, he thought about years past . . .

※

He saw again the years at the lycée in Paris; his parents had wanted him to be a scholar, and the good Norman peasants enriched by the rude métier of cultivation had sent him, finding him solid and intelligent, into the isolation of his Parisian studies. He was said to be as strong in gymnastics as in thematics, and they thought of him for the École Normale. And as he would later form a young man, until sixteen he had remained a very simple fellow, hard-working, honest and religious.

Then, at sixteen, the virile awakening, and the new thoughts, the meditations by which he was amazed, the secret stirring of ancient beliefs; the invasions of novelties and the disturbance of old things; the obscure collision of two spirits; and the muted, slow, tenebrous struggle he could not explain, could not understand; like a newly-awakened sleeper his vision was uncertain and his eyes were blinking.

Another change was also within him; his body became virile. His childhood had been absolutely chaste; in that expansion of good health and regular labor, no impure thought had come to him for a moment; around him, vice swarmed among the pale schoolboys, but it had not attained him, and he was respected for his toil, his bearing, and his simple innocence even more than for the strength of his wrists. So, at sixteen, he was surprised by the development; his humor altered; he sensed vague desires; he perceived that he was no longer the same; he followed, with a furtive astonishment, the progress of growth; two strange ideas assailed him; but he dared not confide in anyone, and nothing instructed him; he only divined that something new, indistinct and monstrous was offered to him, contrary to the former chastity, very confusedly understood.

Thus, that double awakening of the mind and the flesh gradually caused to loom up in his thought the ideas of incredulity and sensuality, faith and chastity. And, anxiously, he addressed himself to God; believing and pure, he gave himself more ardently to religion; and the evangelical breath, from then on, commenced to brush that soul troubled by the elevation of something new and mysterious.

Oh, the day—at sixteen—when he had seen! One Thursday, yes, the day of excursion—it was an afternoon in February—the schoolboys, two by two under the guidance of a study-master, were coming back from the Parc Monceau, chatting among themselves. As he followed an avenue with them, a coupé went past at a trot; he looked; the glasses were raised but, with his good eyes, he could see quite clearly into the interior . . . a man and a woman . . . her tipped back, him, his head inclined over hers, with his arm around her waist . . . he saw them, the man and the woman, enlaced . . .

and very close to the man's breast, the woman's cleavage, breathless beneath her parted corsage, half-naked, white, strangely rounded, frightfully . . . while he respired her breath and she, pressing against his body, contemplated his eyes . . .

Jean Arnaud had seen that. And in the streets of Paris, in the rank of schoolboys, he walked, devoid of thought, sensing follies in his mind, and unknown and bizarre movements in his body, and frissons, with a kind of troubling, wicked enjoyment . . .

Now, on the evening of that day, in the study room illuminated by lamps, in the midst of his comrades, busy or idle, in the warm and blank atmosphere of dictionaries and thinkers, what a dream, O God, he had dreamed! He had understood the two novelties that had loomed up in his mind; he had recognized two things clearly, obscure until then, two things of which books had spoken to him; he recognized the two kinds of concupiscence, the carnal and the spiritual, impurity and incredulity; and the two enemies were revealed to him.

Two roads appeared to him, distinctly, as if they were material, there, before his feet, manifest before his life: spiritual and carnal independence, doubt and pleasure, the mild and easy road to terrestrial life; and sacrifice, spiritual and carnal sacrifice, submission of the spirit, submission of the senses, mortification, silence, violence against oneself, the religious path. The sixteen-year-old innocent, ignorant and free of cares, the simple, naïve and pure individual now saw, suddenly, in the abyss of things, the frightful, inevitable question looms up and he remained haggard, seized by vertigo, on the wooden bench, among his comrades, who were translating Cicero or reading novels in secret.

Pascal's *Pensées*, his favorite book of reasoning and mysticism, was close at hand; he opened it and read . . .

And Jean Arnaud repeated, in the voice of his soul, the unforgettable lines that he had read then . . .

There are many who see that humans have no other enemies than the concupiscence that turns them away from God, not to God but to another wellbeing than God, to the fecund earth: those who believe that human wellbeing is in the flesh, and woe in what turns them away from the pleasures of the senses, in which they intoxicate themselves and of which they die. But those who seek God with all their heart, and who do not have the displeasure of being deprived of his sight, who only have the desire to possess him, and are enemies of those who turn them away, who are afflicted to see themselves surrounded and dominated by such enemies, let them be consoled; I am announcing good news to them: there is a liberator for them; I shall enable them to see him; I shall show them that there is a God for them; I shall not enable them to see the others. I shall enable them to see that a Messiah has been promised who would liberate from enemies, and that one has come to liberate from iniquities, but not from enemies.

Thus, he had looked all around him, and he saw those young men, who would be men, and were men; he no longer distinguished each one; he only perceived the group of those human beings who lived here and there; and he believed that he was seeing the world, the slave of vice, the prey of concupiscence, the miserable vegetating in the flesh and doubt; and he felt an immense commiseration, a limitless compassion, the pity of the crucified, condemned to redeem, doomed to save, fallen in order to rise: the supreme work of universal and eternal salvation. *I shall announce good news to them* . . .

And, illuminated by the splendors of the vocation, he said to himself again, mentally: *Lord, you wanted me; you informed me . . . So be it, my God.*

His resolution had been affirmed in his heart, in the silence of a respected sanctuary, while his mind and his body were those of a man.

His mind embraced things now; he knew literature, and then philosophies and sciences, all the way to Spencer and Haeckel; and all that reasoning philosophy, skeptical, irreligious and, in sum, atheistic, he studied, understanding it without the firmness of his faith being shaken by it. The faith was a sublime edifice in his mind, and everything else a humble appendage or a monument of illusion; he lived in the serene domain of the faith, observing from without the signposts of incredulous philosophies; and amid the turbulence of free examination that surrounded him, only the dogma was stable and precious to his soul.

As resolutely as the sacrifice of thought, he accomplished the sacrifice of the flesh, since the double sacrifice was an absolute condition of the sacerdotal mission. A terrible word haunted him: a single impure memory, Saint-Cyran[1] had said, can trouble a vocation forever.

---

1 The reference is to Jean du Vergier de Hauranne (1681-1643), the superior of a community he founded at Saint-Cyran and the man who introduced Jansenism into France; he was connected with the convent of Port-Royal, mentioned previously, and a significant influence on Blaise Pascal.

And he submitted to the law; full of health and strength, he broke within himself all carnal effort; he folded himself under the Christian rule of virginity.

He pronounced the two renunciations. Thus, little by little, he established mystical and apostolic enthusiasm in his soul, decisively. He only had one occupation, his salvation, and the insistence of that thought already acted on his brain, even alone. He also remained chaste: a young man with a broad brow, black hair, strong lips, powerful muscles, violent nerves, with a warm voice, a fine vibrant chest and ardent blood—yes, such he was—taken entirely by moral labor, he mastered himself, and, not wanting to know sensual pleasures, did not know them.

What became, then, of that sap of burning youth, the power of reproduction, the carnal instinct, the warmth of the blood and the violence of the nerves, the superabundance of life created diabolically to overflow in kisses? The will combated them, tamed them, enchained them, broke them, shredded them; then interrupted in the course of their natural functioning, all his forces were perverted in his body; it was necessary that they be adulterated and, unable to be annihilated, that they go astray and that the workings of that human machine deviate—and that the works of the demon become your work, Lord! So, that flux of animality, compressed, seethed feverishly, and sought, as if desperately, what to be, where to be resolved.

But at that moment, the religious idea filled the brain; the brain lived an intense and exaggerated life therein, and gradually, it absorbed the forces of the organism.

Then, insensibly, it attracted to it the sap of unemployed youth, which flowed through the nerves; the life that ought to have been dispensed in the muscles was concentrated in the brain; muscular life became cerebral life, carnal passion spiritual passion; with the result that the religious idea had exalted the functions of the brain, that the brain had taken possession of the unutilized organic life, and in its turn, the flux of cerebral life, which exhaled from inviolate chastity, excited, stimulated and enfevered religious ardor.

Thus, the organs of thought developed extraordinarily; thus, thankfully, the animal forces degenerated into mysticism: mental force being entirely captured, the force of the senses was corrupted and became mental force, amorous ardor was completely castrated, the generative faculty cursed and condemned to sterility; all life became fever, precipitated in the lobules of thought, absorbed into religion, God; and instead of all the things—pleasures, laughter, tears, intoxications, suffering, enjoyments, long kisses, embraces and violent couplings—instead of those things, amorous dreams, evening dreams, the charms of vague visions, squeezed hands, conversations, whispered words and swoonings of the flesh, instead of the cries and furies of the senses, and the mind, and the victory of the nerves, the blood, the muscles, and the triumph of desire, and anger, and loving, and Hell—instead of all that was not and must not be, there was, dissimulated by the calm appearance of the face, an entirely internal increase of ardor, of religious exaltation, the work of the combined forces of his mind and his flesh, the unique and monstrous function of that powerful organism, perverted by Jesus Christ.

※

And the revelation of the apostolate.

One day, at twenty, he had declared his determination to be a priest, and his resolution, coldly tenacious, remained victorious; on emerging from the antique lycée, he had entered the seminary. At other times, a glance at the comrades who surrounded him had given him an intuition of the apostolate; he reconquered it in his contemplations of the worlds. For, at the end of his studies, gradually, on days of liberty, he commenced long solitary walks in Paris, and after a year of the seminariat, as soon as the doors were opened to him in the first vacation, he resumed his vague strolls; as he had done in his school uniform, and then in his priestly robe, simple and assured, still tall and strong, very grave and pale, he walked alone through Paris, traversing the crowd, without haste, looking round with the eyes of a seer.

By turns, in the aristocratic quarters and the busy quarters of the center where he mingled with crowds, in isolated streets and populous streets, and in the outlying districts where gamins considered him and mocked him from a distance, in crapulous retreats, muddy intersections where girls in rags cast indecent glances at the strength of his muscles, in back streets where people who saw him hesitated to follow him out of fear or shame, he went, calm and tranquil, inhaling the intense breath of the crowd, searching for the secret of the modern life that the lycée had hidden from him and which the seminary hid from him; he went, parading his priestly robe through the ignominious city, amid vices and fevers, placidly, without stopping, straight ahead, like a sleepwalker.

And the evening when his superiors, informed and alarmed, interrogated him; when he appeared, a pale young priest, before his director; when, standing in the light of a window facing the old man, who, looking at him, seemed to divine all the profound things in his soul, he spoke, a humble and certain believer. Yes, his own salvation was very little, but the salvation of others . . . like the apostles, like the Master, the salvation of crowds obsessed him. Oh, the fever born of thought, of desires, of the seething of energies, the fever ignited by the triple furnace of mind, heart and flesh, which was now devouring him!

Thus, the sacred overexcitement, to that degree, was exasperated, so that his religious passion embraced humanity entire; the notion of individuals had been effaced from his soul, in the same way that, long before, considering the young men in the evening study room, he had only perceived a group of human beings moving around him, so, now, he no longer saw anything in the world but the generality of the human species, Christians and pagans, saints and the damned; gradually, common sentiments had been engulfed in the abyss of that vast sensation; particular affections had sunk in the great love of humankind; and, although Christ still loved his mother and his disciple, he, the Apostle, no longer had anything in his heart but an infinite and indistinct love in which God and humanity were mingled in Jesus; he shuddered with pity and tenderness, not for some wretch but for the limitless multitude, the human sinners scattered around him; his thought and his desire embraced the world; his soul wept over evils and smiled at indefinite joys; and the potency of his youth and suffering were exalted for the immensity of the world; disdaining the work of his own salvation, knowing that who saves others saves himself, entirely devoted to charity, he no longer had, before the hallucinated vision of his dream, anything but the folly of universal redemption.

That is why, having known, without being aware of it, the two kinds of concupiscence, he had known, without mingling with it, the society in which the two reigned, and when he went, pensively, through the smoky streets of Paris, he counted the stones of the road where he wanted to walk, measured the boundaries of the empire he wanted to conquer, fixed the site of the palace of truth and light that he had to edify; over swarming humanity he cast the gaze of Hannibal over the Italian camp on the eve of Cannes. Thus, in the midst of men and women, amid the atheistic turbulence, in the gulf of sensualities, sensing the gusts of impiety and lust rising to the tower of his rock, he said to himself, contemplating the vague multitude, penetrating therein, and suffering himself, by virtue of the force of his charity, the essence of his joys and woes, he said to himself, floating indistinctly over those pitiable souls, that the grace of God would give them to him.

※

Later, the novitiate . . .

The shadow of four years in Spain, the studious life and the contemplative life, the austere practices of fasting, prayer, ecstasy and labor, and the sacred monotony of the apostolic preparations.

The confusion, vaguely saintly, of melancholy days . . .

※

So, he had now entered into combat—O joy! O hope of the evangelical mission! The terrible and sublime day was about to dawn. The time had come for the charitable work; the apostolic barriers were open wide; he was setting forth into the world, to preach in the midst of people . . . oh, to march, armed with the Word, through the cities of the world; to sow the name of the living God in the crowds; to plow a strong furrow in those uncultivated souls; to illuminate with warm fecundating splendors those vaults of darkness . . . oh, full of the Spirit, to speak to the masses and to launch into the multitude, like a jet of vapor, the invisible wave of thought . . . to proclaim the master of the Cross, the mystery of the Faith, the joy of Revelation; and in the net of words, to fish the human shoal, like Peter and Paul . . . oh, how sweet then was pain, the suffering, the martyrdom and death—blessed martyrdom, rich suffering, pain transfigured by the radiation of Charity!

O teat of Salvation, mystical fountain of Grace, inexhaustible udder of fertilizations, holy Apostolate: I shall preach the glory of the Lord, I shall announce the News, and I shall evangelize the nations; He will take his elect by His hand, and His breath will be upon hem.

✽

Jean Arnaud preached his first sermon . . . and, ardently loud, his voice enthused souls; the members of the crowd had bowed their heads, some bent their knees, prostrate under the sign of the splendid, enormous, radiant and supernatural cross of the Apostle . . .

Jean Arnaud had preached his first sermon, and, having descended from the pulpit amid the communicant silence of the faithful, he had knelt down on the flagstones in the shadow of the church, motionless, leaning his forehead against a cold wall . . . and he had remained there, as if he were asleep, in a mysterious slumber . . . and when people, approaching him, had touched him, he had made no response; his gaze was vague, his lips parted, his hands limp; he was taken away.

Violent headaches seized him; he had tremors; hot flushes rose to his face; he did not speak; it was as if he had lost his thought. The fever increased; soon there was some nausea; the physician ordered that he be put to bed.

He remained for a week lying in the cell with bare white walls, on a little iron bed surmounted by a huge black crucifix. He had been delirious, and had then had convulsions; gradually, the delirium had eased; now there was a collapse, an apathetic somnolence.

During the day, an old woman presented herself, who said that she was Madame Arnaud. She was taken to her son. Jean Arnaud was lying on the bed, motionless and unconscious; his limbs were stiff; his head was tilted backwards; the veins in his neck, convulsed, resembled thick blue cords; the livid face had dark patches; the eyes, contracted, were two mat black holes in the violet-tinted redness of the conjunctivas; the lower eyelids, blue-tinted, were sagging; the lips were parted by the rictus of the cheek muscles; between the clenched teeth a foamy mucus was oozing; and the entire body lay in a rigid torpor only troubled, increasingly feebly, by the slow and uneven purr of the respiration.

At that moment, the physician came in with the provincial father; he took hold of one of the invalid's arms; the pulse, slow and diminished, was imperceptible; the extremities were icy; the general paralysis was reaching the region of the heart.

It was four o'clock; outside, beyond the casement, the warm summer sun was visible through the branches in the courtyard, in a very pure atmosphere; a few pigeons appeared; sparrows were fluttering and pursuing one another, chirping . . .

Mère Arnaud, motionless and mute, had a confused sensation of the fine countryside where her Jean might have been so tranquil, and so full of beautiful and joyous health; and as her eyes wandered around the moribund's chamber, they saw the great black crucified Christ that was hanging over the head of her child.

A PARTIAL LIST OF SNUGGLY BOOKS

G. ALBERT AURIER *Elsewhere and Other Stories*
S. HENRY BERTHOUD *Misanthropic Tales*
LÉON BLOY *The Desperate Man*
LÉON BLOY *The Tarantulas' Parlor and Other Unkind Tales*
ÉLÉMIR BOURGES *The Twilight of the Gods*
JAMES CHAMPAGNE *Harlem Smoke*
FÉLICIEN CHAMPSAUR *The Latin Orgy*
FÉLICIEN CHAMPSAUR
   The Emerald Princess and Other Decadent Fantasies
BRENDAN CONNELL *Clark*
BRENDAN CONNELL *Jottings from a Far Away Place*
BRENDAN CONNELL *Unofficial History of Pi Wei*
RAFAELA CONTRERAS *The Turquoise Ring and Other Stories*
ADOLFO COUVE *When I Think of My Missing Head*
QUENTIN S. CRISP *Aiaigasa*
QUENTIN S. CRISP *Graves*
LADY DILKE *The Outcast Spirit and Other Stories*
CATHERINE DOUSTEYSSIER-KHOZE *The Beauty of the Death Cap*
BERIT ELLINGSEN *Now We Can See the Moon*
BERIT ELLINGSEN *Vessel and Solsvart*
ENRIQUE GÓMEZ CARRILLO *Sentimental Stories*
EDMOND AND JULES DE GONCOURT *Manette Salomon*
REMY DE GOURMONT *From a Faraway Land*
GUIDO GOZZANO *Alcina and Other Stories*
EDWARD HERON-ALLEN *The Complete Shorter Fiction*
RHYS HUGHES *Cloud Farming in Wales*
J.-K. HUYSMANS *Knapsacks*
COLIN INSOLE *Valerie and Other Stories*
JUSTIN ISIS *Pleasant Tales II*
JUSTIN ISIS (editor) *Marked to Die: A Tribute to Mark Samuels*
JUSTIN ISIS AND DANIEL CORRICK (editors)
   Drowning in Beauty: The Neo-Decadent Anthology

VICTOR JOLY *The Unknown Collaborator and Other Legendary Tales*
MARIE KRYSINSKA *The Path of Amour*
BERNARD LAZARE *The Gate of Ivory*
BERNARD LAZARE *The Mirror of Legends*
BERNARD LAZARE *The Torch-Bearers*
MAURICE LEVEL *The Shadow*
JEAN LORRAIN *Errant Vice*
JEAN LORRAIN *Fards and Poisons*
JEAN LORRAIN *Masks in the Tapestry*
JEAN LORRAIN *Monsieur de Bougrelon and Other Stories*
JEAN LORRAIN *Nightmares of an Ether-Drinker*
JEAN LORRAIN *The Soul-Drinker and Other Decadent Fantasies*
ARTHUR MACHEN *N*
ARTHUR MACHEN *Ornaments in Jade*
CAMILLE MAUCLAIR *The Frail Soul and Other Stories*
CATULLE MENDÈS *Bluebirds*
CATULLE MENDÈS *For Reading in the Bath*
CATULLE MENDÈS *Mephistophela*
ÉPHRAÏM MIKHAËL *Halyartes and Other Poems in Prose*
LUIS DE MIRANDA *Who Killed the Poet?*
OCTAVE MIRBEAU *The Death of Balzac*
TERESA WILMS MONTT *In the Stillness of Marble*
TERESA WILMS MONTT *Sentimental Doubts*
CHARLES MORICE *Babels, Balloons and Innocent Eyes*
DAMIAN MURPHY *Daughters of Apostasy*
DAMIAN MURPHY *The Star of Gnosia*
KRISTINE ONG MUSLIM *Butterfly Dream*
PHILOTHÉE O'NEDDY *The Enchanted Ring*
YARROW PAISLEY *Mendicant City*
URSULA PFLUG *Down From*
ADOLPHE RETTÉ *Misty Thule*
JEAN RICHEPIN *The Bull-Man and the Grasshopper*
DAVID RIX *A Blast of Hunters*
DAVID RIX *A Suite in Four Windows*

FREDERICK ROLFE (Baron Corvo) *Amico di Sandro*
FREDERICK ROLFE (Baron Corvo)
　An Ossuary of the North Lagoon and Other Stories
JASON ROLFE *An Archive of Human Nonsense*
BRIAN STABLEFORD (editor)
　Decadence and Symbolism: A Showcase Anthology
BRIAN STABLEFORD (editor) *The Snuggly Satyricon*
BRIAN STABLEFORD *The Insubstantial Pageant*
BRIAN STABLEFORD *Spirits of the Vasty Deep*
BRIAN STABLEFORD *The Truths of Darkness*
COUNT ERIC STENBOCK *Love, Sleep & Dreams*
COUNT ERIC STENBOCK *Myrtle, Rue & Cypress*
COUNT ERIC STENBOCK *The Shadow of Death*
COUNT ERIC STENBOCK *Studies of Death*
MONTAGUE SUMMERS *The Bride of Christ and Other Fictions*
GILBERT-AUGUSTIN THIERRY *The Blonde Tress and The Mask*
GILBERT-AUGUSTIN THIERRY *Reincarnation and Redemption*
DOUGLAS THOMPSON *The Fallen West*
TOADHOUSE *Gone Fishing with Samy Rosenstock*
TOADHOUSE *Living and Dying in a Mind Field*
RUGGERO VASARI *Raun*
JANE DE LA VAUDÈRE *The Demi-Sexes and The Androgynes*
JANE DE LA VAUDÈRE *The Double Star and Other Occult Fantasies*
JANE DE LA VAUDÈRE *The Mystery of Kama and Brahma's Courtesans*
JANE DE LA VAUDÈRE *The Priestesses of Mylitta*
JANE DE LA VAUDÈRE *Syta's Harem and Pharaoh's Lover*
JANE DE LA VAUDÈRE *Three Flowers and The King of Siam's Amazon*
JANE DE LA VAUDÈRE *The Witch of Ecbatana and The Virgin of Israel*
AUGUSTE VILLIERS DE L'ISLE-ADAM *Isis*
RENÉE VIVIEN AND HÉLÈNE DE ZUYLEN DE NYEVELT
　Faustina and Other Stories
RENÉE VIVIEN *Lilith's Legacy*
RENÉE VIVIEN *A Woman Appeared to Me*
KAREL VAN DE WOESTIJNE *The Dying Peasant*

Lightning Source UK Ltd.
Milton Keynes UK
UKHW040645120220
358601UK00002B/407